#4 Who Framed Mary Bubnik?

Look for these and other books
in the Bad News Ballet series:

#1 *The Terrible Tryouts*
#2 *Battle of the Bunheads*
#3 *Stupid Cupids*
#4 *Who Framed Mary Bubnik?*

#4 Who Framed Mary Bubnik?

Jahnna N. Malcolm

SCHOLASTIC INC.
New York Toronto London Auckland Sydney

FOR OUR SIBLINGS (IN ORDER OF APPEARANCE)
DEL HILLGARTNER, CHARLIE BEECHAM, AND
DEBBIE HILLGARTNER

ISBN 0-590-42472-6

12 11 10 9 8 7 6 5 4 9/8 0 1 2 3 4/9

Printed in the U.S.A. 11

First Scholastic printing, August 1989

Chapter One

"I've got some truly wonderful news!" Zan Reed called as she skipped down the street to meet her friends. They were sitting on the front steps of Hillberry Hall, where the Deerfield Academy of Dance had its studios.

"What? Has ballet class been canceled?" Gwendolyn Hayes took a large slurp of the ice-cream cone she held in her hand. "Now *that* would be good news."

Kathryn McGee, who was sitting beside her, giggled and nearly lost the top scoop of chocolate-marshmallow ice cream off of her cone.

"Careful," Gwen warned. "Once the ice cream hits

the sidewalk it's really hard getting all the gravel out of it."

McGee stared at her friend. "You wouldn't *really* eat it if it hit the ground, would you?"

The short pudgy redhead shrugged and took another lick of her cone. "I might. If no one was looking."

McGee made a face and flipped one of her chestnut braids over her shoulder. "That's gross."

They watched as their friend Zan raced up to them and leaned against the metal railing to catch her breath. "I ran all the way." She took off her lavender beret and fanned her face with it. "I can hardly talk."

McGee had never seen Zan so excited before. Normally she was quiet and painfully shy. Patting the step beside her, McGee said, "Sit down and tell us what the good news is."

The thin black girl smiled at Gwen and McGee, then pulled a long envelope out of her pocket. She held it up like a special treasure. "This came in the mail today."

Gwen pushed her wire-rimmed glasses up on her nose and peered at the writing on the outside of the light pink letter. "It says, 'From Tiffany Truenote — Confidential.' "

"Isn't she the detective in those books you read?" McGee asked.

"Yes!" Zan nodded and her brown eyes sparkled with excitement. "Can you believe it?"

Gwen, who had finished both scoops of her chocolate ice cream, nearly choked on the sugar cone. "I didn't know she was a real person."

Zan laughed. "She's not. But the publishers of her books are holding a special contest." She waved the envelope in the air. "And this is my application form, and the rules."

"What kind of contest?" McGee leaned forward, with her elbows on her knees. She loved contests, particularly athletic ones.

" 'It's a mystery to me,' " Zan said.

Gwen cocked her head. "What is? Life?"

"No." Zan opened the envelope and held up the entry form. "That's the name of the contest." She stood up and paced back and forth on the sidewalk. "You see, we're supposed to solve a mystery in our home town, then write about it. The person with the best mystery wins two hundred dollars and two autographed books from the author."

"Geez Louise!" McGee gasped. "Just for writing a mystery?"

"A *true* mystery. It has to be from real life." Suddenly the light faded from Zan's eyes. She slumped down on the steps and moaned, "Unfortunately, nothing truly mysterious ever happens here in Deerfield, Ohio."

"Why don't you just make one up?" Gwen asked, sneaking a lick of McGee's ice cream. "They'd never know."

"I couldn't do that!" Zan stared at Gwen in shock. "That would be dishonest. Besides, it has to be signed by two witnesses verifying it as the truth."

"OK, what about this?" Gwen suggested. "On Thursdays my school serves this strange loaf made out of stuff that all the sixth-graders call 'mystery meat.' You figure out what that stuff is, and you'll win the contest for sure."

Zan laughed. "We have the same thing." She lived right in downtown Deerfield and was in the fifth grade at Stewart Elementary.

Gwen stole another big bite of ice cream off of McGee's cone.

"I'll give you a mystery that's pretty easy to solve," McGee said.

"What?" Zan's eyes widened.

"The case of the disappearing ice cream." McGee looked down at the empty cone in her hand. "One minute I have a scoop of Rocky Road, and the next minute it's gone."

Zan and McGee turned to look at Gwen, who had a large chocolate smudge on her cheek. "I wonder who could have done it?"

"Hey, I was just trying to help," Gwen protested. "You had Rocky Road running down your arm. Pretty soon the whole thing would have melted."

McGee narrowed her green eyes at her friend. "Don't do me any more favors, OK?"

Gwen chuckled nervously, then changed the subject. "Speaking of Rocky — wasn't she supposed to meet us here?"

Zan nodded. "We all agreed to meet before ballet class for ice cream cones. But I was late and missed the ice cream."

"Don't feel bad," McGee cracked. "I was *here* and missed it."

Gwen pointedly ignored McGee's remark and peered down the street. "Rocky usually takes the bus in from the base. Maybe her dad drove her today."

Rochelle Garcia's father was a sergeant stationed at Curtiss-Dobbs Air Force base just outside Deerfield. She and her four brothers lived on the base, and Rocky attended sixth grade there.

McGee checked her watch. "Well, she'd better hurry 'cause ballet class starts in fifteen minutes."

"And what about Mary Bubnik?" Zan asked. "Where's she?"

"Oh, she's always late," McGee said, with a wave of her hand.

Gwen nodded in agreement, her short straight hair bobbing up and down. "Mr. Toad probably broke down again."

"Mr. Toad?" McGee raised an eyebrow.

"Right," Gwen said. "That run-down old car her mother drives is always dying on the street somewhere."

As if in answer, a car backfired loudly on the street in front of them. The girls looked up to see an ancient green Volvo lurch to a halt by the curb. The passenger door swung open and a blonde, curly headed fifth-grader hopped out.

Zan, McGee, and Gwen leaped to their feet. "Mary, we're over here," Zan cried.

Mary Bubnik didn't seem to hear them. She raced up the marble steps to the big glass doors of Hillberry Hall, stopping once to blow her nose loudly with a tissue. Her shoulders were hunched over, and she kept the tissue pressed tightly to her face.

"Hey, Mary!" McGee shouted as she took the stairs two at a time.

"Wait for us!" Zan was right behind her.

"I wonder if she has a cold," Gwen called after them from the foot of the steps. She scooped up her hat and pink parka, searched for her gloves, then struggled to get her dance bag on her shoulder. By the time she had gathered all her belongings together, Zan and McGee had caught up with Mary Bubnik.

"What's the matter, Mary?" Zan asked softly. "Are you OK?"

Mary Bubnik shook her head. She blinked her big blue eyes, trying to speak, then covered her face with her tissue. Zan and McGee exchanged worried looks.

They didn't need to be detectives to know that something was terribly wrong. Mary Bubnik had been crying.

"What's going on?" Gwen called as she huffed

her way up the one hundred and two steps to the pillared entrance of the building. "Did someone die?"

Mary buried her head in her hands. "Worse!"

"Someone's *going* to die?" Zan clutched Mary Bubnik's arm.

Mary nodded and blubbered, "Me. My mom says we can't afford any more dance classes. This is my last month. I know I'll never see you guys again, and that'll just kill me!"

Chapter Two

"This is terrible!" Rocky Garcia shouted when she heard the news. She had joined the girls who were clustered in the front lobby of Hillberry Hall. "We can't let it happen."

Zan nodded emphatically. "I'm truly certain we can work something out."

"I'll die if I can't see you all," Mary Bubnik drawled in her soft southern accent. "I'll just die."

"Look, even if you can't take dance classes," McGee said, trying to be logical, "we can still get together."

Mary Bubnik shook her head. "It wouldn't be the same, you know that. We all go to different schools."

"She's right," Rocky said. "When all of us met in

December we decided to take these dance classes just so we would be sure to stick together."

Gwen nodded. "We've been meeting here for three months, and it sure hasn't been because we like ballet."

"I can see it all now," Mary Bubnik whimpered in between little hiccuping sobs. "Every Saturday you guys will be having all that fun in dance class, and pretty soon you'll just forget about me."

"That's not true!" Zan declared, offering Mary her hankie.

"Besides, who said we were having fun in dance class?" Gwen quipped.

Rocky punched Gwen on the shoulder. "Get serious. We've got to figure out a way for Mary to save some money."

"Mom says we have to tighten our belts and cut out all luxuries. She's giving up the gym, and I have to give up ballet." Mary Bubnik blew her nose loudly. "Nothing's the way it used to be."

Mary's parents had split up the previous summer. In September she and her mother had moved from Oklahoma to Ohio. The big change had been hard on both of them.

She pulled a wrinkled check out of the pocket of her faded down parka. It was made out to the Deerfield Academy. "See? This is already two weeks late. They're probably going to yell at me."

"We'll go with you to the office." Rocky snapped

up her red satin jacket. "And if anybody yells at you, they get a fist sandwich from me."

Mary's blue eyes were two huge circles. "Even Mr. Anton?"

Rocky hesitated. Mr. Anton was the director of the ballet academy and very strict. Even the older students were intimidated by him. Rocky squared her shoulders and declared, "Even him. I'll punch holes in his tights."

Mary Bubnik couldn't help giggling, and that made everyone feel better. Mary usually looked on the bright side of things, with something nice to say about everyone, so when she was down, that brought the whole gang down.

"Come on!" McGee led them up the stairs to the third floor. "I'll bet Mr. Anton isn't even here today. It's probably Miss Delacorte, and she's nice."

"Thanks, you guys," Mary murmured. "This is so embarrassing."

McGee patted Mary Bubnik on the arm. "It could happen to anyone."

"Don't give up hope," Zan chimed in. "You know what they say — it's always darkest before the dawn."

"Who says that?" McGee asked.

Zan shrugged her thin shoulders. "*They* do."

McGee raised an eyebrow. "*They* say a lot of things."

"Well, I wish *they'd* put an elevator in this building." Gwen threw herself dramatically against the wall of the second floor landing. "I think I'm going to have a heart attack."

"Come on, hurry." McGee tugged at Gwen's arm. "Or we'll all get yelled at for being late to class."

Gwen held up one hand in protest. "I have to take a break. I think I ate my ice cream too fast."

McGee put her hands on her hips. "You mean, *my* ice cream."

Gwen sat down on the marble step and unzipped her blue dance bag with the pink ballet slippers on it. She shifted her stash of corn chips, M&Ms, and Twinkies, then pulled out a can of diet 7-up. She popped off the top and took two quick gulps.

"I can't believe you," Rocky exclaimed.

"Yeah," McGee said, "how can you eat anything else?"

"I'm not eating," Gwen snapped. "I'm drinking this to settle my stomach." She held the can out in front of her. "Anybody want some?"

"No way," Rocky retorted. "Then we'd just slosh around on the dance floor." She raced ahead to the third floor and peered in through the door leading to the Academy of Dance. She tiptoed back to the stairs and called, "Come on, everybody, Miss Delacorte's at her desk."

As the gang entered the reception area they were greeted by a loud shriek, followed by the words, "Suck in your stomach! Stand up straight! Lock those knees. Reee-laaax!"

Gwen nearly spilled the remains of her soda as she tried to follow orders. It took several seconds for her to realize the words were coming from the big black bird perched on Miss Delacorte's shoulder.

"Now, now, Miss Myna," the aging receptionist cooed to the bird. "You will have to be quiet when we are work-ink, yes?"

The bird cocked its head to one side. "My lips are sealed." Then it shrieked, "Seals! Brawk! Bring on the seals!"

Mary Bubnik clapped her hands together in delight. "Where did you get that wonderful bird?"

"Miss Myna was in zee circus," Miss Delacorte replied in her Russian accent. "When she became too talky, I was given her. We've been together for . . . oh, let me think — ten years now."

"Ten years!" McGee repeated. "How come we've never seen her before?"

"She doesn't like the cold winters," Miss Delacorte explained, stroking the bird along its beak. "So for those months she stays home with the rest of my animals." Miss Delacorte held her finger up to her shoulder and the bird stepped onto it. Then she set Miss Myna on the desk and the bird paced back and forth, pecking at rubber bands and paper clips. "Now that spring is here, she insisted on com-ink to work with me. Just like Rudi. They get lonely."

"Rudi?" Zan repeated. "Who's that?"

"I will show you." Miss Delacorte bent over and

peered under her desk, where a large wire cage had been placed. "Oh, dear, that little rascal has gotten out of his house again." She shook her head. "Mr. Anton won't like that at all. Rudi!" She whistled softly, and Miss Myna answered her.

The girls moved closer to the desk, and the bird fluffed up its feathers in alarm. "Back up, folks!" Miss Myna crowed. "I need a little breathing room. Brawk!"

"Miss Myna, be nice," Miss Delacorte scolded gently. "Don't be such a czarina!"

"What's a czarina?" McGee asked.

"Is Russian for empress," Miss Delacorte explained. "Rudi!" she called once more, then shrugged. "Oh, well, he'll be back when he gets hungry." Before the girls could ask what kind of animal Rudi was, Miss Delacorte folded her hands in front of her and asked, "Now, what can I do for you?"

Mary's laughter quickly died as she dug in her pocket for the check. "I'm here to pay for my lessons. I'm really sorry for being late."

Miss Delacorte waved her purple scarf in the air. "It is all right. As long as it doesn't become a habit." She pulled open the top drawer of her desk and rifled through it. "I will give you a receipt."

The girls watched as Miss Delacorte searched through the papers on top of her desk, making sure to avoid Miss Myna's beak. Then one by one she searched the drawers. A perplexed look came over the old lady's face.

"What's the matter, Miss Delacorte?" Zan asked.

"The receipt book. I cannot find it." The tiny lady turned in a circle, searching through the in/out mail piles, the wastebasket, and back through each desk drawer. She even opened her purse and looked there.

Miss Myna picked up on her words and croaked, "Receipt! Receipt! Reeee-laaaaxxxxx!"

"Why does Miss Myna keep saying, 'Reeee-laaaaxxxxx'? " Mary Bubnik asked.

"I leave television on for her each morning," Miss Delacorte replied. "She listens to a program on yoga."

"Maybe you put your receipt book in your cash box," Zan said.

Miss Delacorte clapped her hands together. "Of course! That would be the perfect spot for it. Silly me!"

The girls watched as she began her search all over again. This one was more frantic. She wrung her hands muttering, "It has to be here. I just had it." Finally she stood up and moved to the file cabinet in the corner. "That box had the entire week's money in it, and now it has disappeared into thin ice."

"I think you mean thin air," Gwen corrected as the girls gathered around the desk trying to help.

Miss Delacorte pressed one palm to her forehead.

"I don't know what is happen-ink these days. I write myself notes — they disappear. And now I lose every-think — Rudi, the receipt book, and worst of all, the cash box."

"Think back to the last time you had the cash box," Zan said. "Were you in this room? Who paid the last bill?" As she spoke, Zan pulled out her lavender pad to take notes. She found it always helped to figure things out if she wrote them down.

Miss Delacorte tapped her head. "I can't think. My brain has gone — how do you say? — empty."

"Try going through the actions of what you did last," Zan suggested. "Sometimes your body will remember where things are even if your mind can't."

"Where'd you hear that?" Rocky asked.

"Tiffany Truenote uses that technique in several of her books," Zan said, patting the pocket that held the entry form. She was already getting into a "detective" mode.

Meanwhile, Miss Delacorte was silently miming the action of taking money and putting it in a box. Zan wrote down how she did it, then asked, "Did you go anywhere today?"

"Not that I can remember."

"Not even lunch?" Gwen added.

"I eat here." Miss Delacorte put her head in her hands. "Oh, dear, this is not work-ink."

"Just give it a try," Mary Bubnik said. "Zan's usually right about these things. She's awfully smart."

Miss Delacorte shook her head. "I've been sitt-ink here all morn-ink. I only got up once to go to the ladies' room to check my lipstick. That's all."

"That's it!" Zan cried. The girls scampered across the lobby to the bathroom, practically knocking Miss Delacorte down in their excitement.

Zan swung open the door and, sure enough, the cash box was perched right on the edge of the sink.

"Oh, how wonderful!" Miss Delacorte cried, swooping the box up in her arms like a lost baby.

"And that shows you what careful deduction can do," Zan declared proudly.

"Zan wants to be a detective," Mary Bubnik whispered to Miss Delacorte, "just like her hero, Tiffany Truenote."

Miss Delacorte hugged the cash box to her chest. "I hope you succeed." She gave Zan an affectionate squeeze. "You certainly helped me solve this mystery."

A sudden burst of piano music from Studio A made the girls all jump at once. McGee checked her watch and said, "Wow. We'd better hurry, if we're going to get changed and to class on time."

Mary Bubnik suddenly felt sad all over again. "Yeah, I wouldn't want to be late for one of my last classes."

"Last class?" Miss Delacorte asked. "What nonsense are you talk-ink?"

Mary bit her lower lip. "I'm afraid this is going to be my last month at the academy." Her voice cracked as she said, "My mom can't afford my lessons anymore."

"Now isn't that just too bad!" a voice sang out from behind them.

The girls spun to see Courtney Clay standing with her arms crossed, grinning at them. She was already dressed in her black leotard and pink tights, her dark hair pulled into a tight knot on top of her head. "One down," Courtney said sweetly, "four to go."

"What's that supposed to mean?"McGee asked.

"It means that everything is working just as I'd hoped. First Mary Bubnik will have to go, and then all of you will follow."

"Mary, don't listen to her," Gwen hissed. "She's just a Bunhead."

"Yeah." Rocky glared at Courtney and pushed the sleeves of her jacket up. "And it's time to teach this Bunhead a lesson."

"You stay away from me, Rocky Garcia," Courtney warned as she backed toward the studio. "Fighting's not allowed here."

"Where does it say that?" Rocky moved in closer. "I don't see any signs."

"It's a rule," Courtney replied shrilly. "My mother said so." Courtney's mother was on the board of the Deerfield Academy of Dance, and Courtney never let anyone forget it.

"Girls, please behave yourselves!" Miss Delacorte said sternly. "This is a ballet studio."

"You don't have to tell me that." Courtney pointed to Rocky. "Tell her and her poor, penniless friend." She turned on her heel and flounced toward the studio but paused just long enough to whisper to Mary Bubnik, "I'm glad you're leaving. None of us real dancers will miss you."

Mary felt like she had been slapped in the face. The tears she had managed to control before suddenly sprang to her eyes. Covering her face with her hands, she ran for the bathroom.

Gwen turned to follow Mary but Zan grabbed her arm. "Let her go. She probably needs to be alone right now."

Rocky murmured darkly, "Nobody is mean to my friends and lives to tell about it."

"Come on, Rocky," Zan urged, "we have more important things to worry about than a silly old Bunhead."

"Like what?" McGee demanded. She was ready to join Rocky in her fight against Courtney.

Zan looked over her shoulder to where Mary Bubnik had disappeared. "We need to come up with a way to get money for Mary."

Chapter Three

The changing room looked bright and cheery after the long winter months. The two windows had been opened wide and a fresh spring breeze blew through the curtains into the small room but the girls didn't feel very springlike. Their friend was in trouble, and they didn't know how to help.

Gwen quickly stepped behind the free-standing mirror to change, making sure that no one could see her. Gwen had a few hard and fast rules that she lived by. One of them was never let *anyone* see you in your underwear — even your own mother.

Rocky changed into her leotard and tights and then yanked her wild, dark hair into a side ponytail. Zan, who already had her dance clothes on under her navy corduroy jumper, stood waiting for the group by the dressing room exit. McGee pulled on her faded black leotard over a pair of tights with runs in them and joined Zan and Rocky.

"You guys wait up." Gwen staggered out from behind the mirror, clutching her outfit. "I can't get my leotard on. I think it shrunk."

McGee arched an eyebrow at Gwen's plump form, but didn't say anything.

"Should we wait for Mary?" Zan asked the group.

"Naw," Rocky said. "She'll come when she's ready."

"Welcome!" Annie Springer cried as the girls filed into Studio B. "Welcome, everyone." Their teacher stood smiling by the tall windows at the end of the room. Sunlight streamed through the glass, filling the room with a golden glow. "It looks like spring is finally here," she said with a giggle. "I thought winter would never end."

"The sun comes out for one day," Gwen whispered to McGee, "and everyone's buying suntan lotion."

Annie, who was wearing a black leotard and short black wraparound skirt, skipped over to the piano. "Mrs. Bruce, would you play something light and airy in honor of this first day of spring?"

"With pleasure." The plump old accompanist began playing a lively tune, and the heavy folds of skin on her arms jiggled merrily in time to the music.

"Perfect!" Annie cried. She turned to the girls who were standing by the ballet *barre* waiting to begin their warm-ups. "Class, let's skip our *pliés* and *relevées* today."

"That's OK with me," Rocky murmured gratefully. "I was getting pretty tired of the same old bend your knees and straighten 'em routine."

Annie clapped her hands together. "Step away from the *barre,* everyone, and give yourself plenty of room to move."

"Let's stand in front," Courtney said to her friends Page Tuttle and Alice Wescott. Page was a tall, slender blonde with a short, turned-up nose. Alice, who was only a fourth-grader, was thin and mousy. Each was dressed in the studio uniform of pink tights and a black leotard, their hair pulled back tightly in a bun on their heads. The three of them paraded by with their chins held high, their feet turned out in an exaggerated dancer's walk.

"Get a load of the Bunheads," McGee cracked. "They look like ducks."

The gang moved away from the *barre,* making sure to stay at the back of the room. Zan looked anxiously toward the door but there was no sign of Mary Bubnik.

"Now, girls, I want you to let yourselves go with the music. Pretend you are leaves floating along on the spring breeze."

"Gimme a break," Gwen grumbled beneath her breath.

Annie swayed dreamily in front of them, then spun around in a lazy circle. She scurried across the room in tiny, little steps.

Courtney and the Bunheads immediately began to imitate Annie, each trying to outdo the other in their graceful flutterings.

The gang stood together in a line rocking from one foot to the other. Zan, who had been quiet since class began, suddenly whispered, "I've got it! I'm going to win the Tiffany Truenote contest. And when I get the prize money I'll give it to Mary Bubnik."

"But what if you don't win?" Gwen asked.

"Then we'll all chip in and pay for her lessons," Rocky replied. "I've got about five dollars saved right now."

"What if we all saved our lunch money?" McGee suggested.

"Lunch money!" Gwen shouted. She clapped her hand over her mouth as Annie Springer looked over in her direction. To make sure their teacher thought she was dancing, Gwen raised up on her toes and *bourréed* around her friends, flapping her arms in her best imitation of a bird.

"You mean, not eat lunch?" Gwen hissed the moment Annie looked away. "I don't think I could do that. I'd never make it through math and geography. I'd be too faint."

Rocky imitated Gwen, trotting behind her with flapping arms. "Couldn't you give up lunch just for one week? I mean, it's for a friend."

"Yeah," McGee chimed in, joining the line as she waved her arms up and down. "This is serious."

"You're telling me," Gwen said. "A whole week without food — "

"No one said you had to go without food." Zan fluttered up beside Gwen. "You could secretly pack a sandwich to take with you. Just don't buy lunch."

"Hey, that's not a bad idea." Gwen led them all in a wide, swooping circle. "I could make a couple of sandwiches, bring some bananas, an apple or two, a couple of bags of chips, some cookies — and I'd be just fine."

"Fine? You'd be dead," Rocky exclaimed. "Nobody could eat that much."

"Want to bet?"

"Oh, look, class," Annie called out. "A flock of geese!"

Gwen's knees locked and Rocky, Zan, and McGee piled into her back. They craned their heads around, searching for whoever was doing bird dances.

"I don't see any geese," McGee whispered.

"That's because Annie was referring to us," Gwen hissed back. Most of the class members were staring while the Bunheads pointed at them and snickered.

"Those guys are asking for it," Rocky grumbled.

The music shifted to a faster tempo and Annie

shouted, "Now pretend that you're fairies, coming out to celebrate the coming of spring." Annie demonstrated by doing a *grand jeté,* soaring high up into the air before landing lightly on her feet.

"Fairies?" Rocky said, watching Courtney and several of the other dancers in the class flit around the room. "No way."

The door creaked open and Mary Bubnik tiptoed into the studio. Her face was shiny from being scrubbed but that was the only sign that she had been crying. She smiled at the gang and quickly joined them. "What did I miss?"

"A parade of ducks," Gwen said, pointing at the Bunheads.

"And a herd of geese." McGee gestured to Rocky, Zan, and Gwen.

"Don't you mean a flock of geese?" Zan corrected.

Gwen shook her head. "The way we were dancing, I think herd is more accurate."

"Now we're supposed to be fairies," Zan explained, "celebrating spring's arrival."

The studio was swirling with movement as all the girls circled the room, doing running leaps and jumps.

"That looks like fun!" Mary dove into the crowd going by and threw herself into the exercise. As she ran, Mary cried, "Run, run — *leap!*" The next time she passed the gang, Mary called out, "Come on!"

Rocky shrugged. "If you can't beat 'em, join 'em."

With a delighted howl she bounded into the center of the room, doing her highest karate kick. The others followed suit.

"Hey," Gwen said, landing with a thud, "this *is* kind of fun!"

" 'Specially if you add the yell," Rocky advised. "Haiee!"

McGee jumped straight up in the air and spun in a circle. "Yippee!" Several of their classmates took up her cry and soon everyone was leaping and whooping with joy.

When Mrs. Bruce hit the final chord the girls collapsed in a heap on the floor, gasping for breath and giggling deliriously.

Annie, who was out of breath herself, led the group in a final curtsy. "Thank you, everyone. That was marvelous."

When she straightened up, Annie said, "Next week we'll have to go back to our usual exercises, but for today — go outside and have a wonderful weekend!"

Courtney Clay and the Bunheads were the first to reach the studio door. They paused just long enough to give the gang a disdainful look.

"Careful, Clay," Rocky warned. "Your face might get stuck that way."

Courtney stuck out her tongue and flounced out of the room. Page and Alice trotted right behind her.

"Boy," McGee huffed, "I wish all of our dance classes were like that."

"Me, too." Mary Bubnik smiled wistfully. "It almost makes you forget about your troubles."

"Speaking of troubles," Zan said, giving Mary a big smile, "I think we've come up with a solution for yours."

"What?" Mary looked eagerly from face to face.

"We're all going to chip in and pay for your lessons," McGee declared.

Gwen beamed proudly. "We're even using our lunch money."

"Y'all are so sweet." Mary Bubnik could feel tears welling up again, and she fought hard to keep them back. "But I could never take any money from you. My mom wouldn't let me. She's too proud."

Zan looked at the others and then patted Mary Bubnik gently on the back. "Well, then we'll just have to think of another way to get the money."

Suddenly a bloodcurdling scream split the air. It came from the direction of the dressing room and the gang raced toward the sound.

"Robbed!" Courtney's unmistakable voice shrieked. "I've been robbed!"

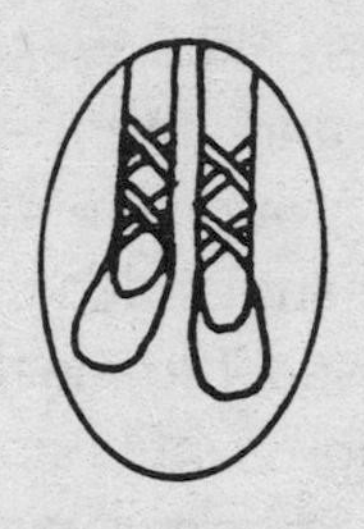

Chapter Four

"Everybody, up against the wall!"

Courtney barked her command so powerfully that all the girls in the dressing room obeyed. Courtney crossed her arms across her chest and glared at the lineup. "I had a twenty-four-carat gold chain, with a twenty-four-carat gold dancer hanging from it. It was a special gift from my mother, who is the president of the board of this ballet academy. I know for certain that it was in my bag before class started." She gestured toward her sleek nylon dance bag lying open on the dressing table. "And now it's gone. Somebody stole it!"

"Are you sure you left it in your bag?" Mary Bubnik asked meekly.

"Of course I'm sure. I put it in the same side pocket every time." She held out her hand and snapped her fingers. Alice Wescott leaped to hand her the dance bag, and Courtney displayed the ransacked bag to the group. The usually neat bag had legwarmers and toeshoes dangling sloppily over the sides. Courtney tossed it to the floor in disgust. "Nobody leaves this room until I find out who did it."

Just then Annie Springer came through the curtain to see what the commotion was all about. "What's going on in here?"

"Somebody stole my gold necklace," Courtney replied. "And I want it back!"

"Are you sure it's stolen?" Annie asked. "Maybe you dropped it in the studio accidentally."

"Never!" Courtney shook her head vehemently. "I always keep it in my dance bag during class."

"Have you looked in the studio?" Annie persisted.

"No," Courtney admitted.

"I'll go check, just in case." Annie darted back through the curtain as the rest of the girls whispered nervously together.

Rocky, who had been shocked to silence by Courtney's outburst, finally found her voice. "Listen, Courtney, what makes you think anyone would want your dumb necklace, anyway?"

"I can think of *someone* in this room who could use a twenty-four-carat gold necklace." Courtney walked down the line of girls until she stood right in front of Mary Bubnik. "Someone who's so poor her mother can't even afford to buy her a pair of ballet shoes that fit."

Mary stared down at her big floppy dance shoes. She had to stuff tissue paper into the toes to make them stay on her feet. Right then and there, Mary Bubnik vowed never to wear those shoes again, even if her mother did find a way to pay for her dance classes.

"Someone who knows that my necklace is worth three months worth of ballet lessons." Courtney narrowed her eyes at Mary Bubnik.

"Just hold it right there, Courtney Clay!" McGee sprang to Mary's defense. "If you're accusing somebody of stealing, just say it out loud. Quit pussyfooting around."

"She doesn't have to say my name," Mary Bubnik cried, her eyes filling with tears. "Everybody knows who she's talking about!"

"You'd better have some proof," Zan declared.

"Yeah, if Mary took your necklace," Gwen demanded, "where'd she put it?"

"The same place she put my two Snickers bars," Courtney retorted.

"Snickers bars?" Page Tuttle gasped in shock. "Courtney, how could you?"

"You're always telling us a dancer never eats junk food," Alice Wescott whined in her thin nasal voice.

Courtney spun to face her friends. "I carry them for a quick energy pickup whenever I've had a particularly strenuous workout in class. That's all."

"Yes, but *two* candy bars?" Page exclaimed.

"Oh, forget the candy bars!" Courtney shouted. "What about my necklace?"

"If I was missing two Snickers bars," Gwen observed, "I'd start looking for an overweight ballerina."

The entire roomful of girls turned to stare at Gwen's pudgy form.

"Not me!" she protested hurriedly. "I've got my own supplies. I don't need anyone else's."

"I wouldn't put stealing past any of you losers," Courtney declared.

"Who're you calling a loser?" Rocky snapped. "You better watch your mouth, or I'll — "

"Or you'll what, you — you J.D.!" Courtney challenged. "Don't think I've forgotten who threatened me before class today."

Rocky looked confused. She whispered to McGee out the side of her mouth, "What's a J.D.?"

"Juvenile delinquent," McGee hissed.

"Oh. *What?*"

McGee grabbed Rocky by the arm before she could do anything drastic.

"Come on," Gwen declared, looping her arm in Mary Bubnik's and turning to leave. "We don't have to stick around here and be insulted."

"Hold it!" Courtney shrieked. "I said, *nobody*

leaves this room until I get my necklace back — and I mean it!"

Before the gang could protest Courtney snapped her fingers at Page. "Get Mr. Anton right now. He'll get to the bottom of this. And while you're at it, call the police!"

"The police? Oh, no!" Mary Bubnik's eyes were wide with panic. "I'm sure your necklace is here someplace. It must have fallen out onto the floor."

"Look at her!" Alice Wescott cried, pointing triumphantly. "Mary Bubnik's scared to death. That's a sure sign she did it."

Courtney turned to face the rest of the girls in the class, who'd been huddling in the corner. "Everyone had better check their bags. I'll bet more stuff is missing. When Mr. Anton gets here with the police, you can report it, too."

Mary Bubnik turned to her friends. "What are we going to do?"

"Relax," Rocky said confidently. "My dad's a security policeman. I know how these things work. They've got nothing on us."

"Remember, we're innocent until proven guilty," Zan said, squeezing Mary's hand.

The curtain moved and Miss Delacorte fluttered into the room. Her myna bird was perched on her left shoulder and in her right hand she clutched a piece of yellow paper. "My goodness, what is happen-ink?"

"Where's Mr. Anton?" Courtney demanded, putting her hands on her hips.

"He's in class right now," Miss Delacorte answered. "But perhaps I can help you."

"OK. I want to report a theft. My necklace was stolen, and one of these girls took it." She gestured with her thumb to Mary and the gang. "I want you to frisk them."

"I can't do that!" Miss Delacorte replied.

"Then have the police do it."

"I can't call the police."

"Why not?"

"Because I don't know the number, and even if I did, I wouldn't know what to tell them."

"Oooh! That is just typical of you!" Courtney exploded. "You can't do anything right, you senile old bat!"

The old lady recoiled in shock. Miss Myna rared up and flapped her wings. Miss Delacorte set the paper in her hand on the dressing table and tried to calm the bird, petting it along its bill.

"And that stupid bird is a nuisance and a health hazard," Courtney ranted. "I can't believe it. My precious necklace has been stolen, and you're not going to do a thing about it."

Miss Delacorte focused her pale blue eyes on Courtney in confusion. "How can you say such things?"

"You're deliberately protecting these thieves. Well,

I'm telling my mother, and she'll have you fired!"

"Courtney!" Annie Springer cried from the doorway. "That's no way to talk to Miss Delacorte. I think you owe her an apology."

Courtney tilted up her chin defiantly. "I can say whatever I want. Where's my necklace? Did you find it in the studio?"

"No," Annie said coldly. "But I'm sure it's here somewhere."

Courtney snatched up her dance bag. "I'm going to find Mr. Anton. He'll call the police." Alice and Page fell in line behind her, and they stomped out of the dressing room.

"Oh, Miss Delacorte," Annie said, rushing to comfort the old woman, "I'm so sorry you had to endure that."

"It is all right," Miss Delacorte replied. "Courtney is very upset right now. I'm sure she didn't mean what she said." Miss Delacorte shook her head sadly. "But she is right, I am so forgetful these days."

"Now, don't say that!" Annie said quickly. "We all forget things from time to time." A worried frown crossed her face. "But I think we must talk to Mr. Anton about this. Thefts in the studio are very, very serious." Annie looked up at the rest of the girls in the dressing room. "I'm sure this has all been a misunderstanding. But, just to be on the safe side, watch your belongings, girls. And don't bring anything valuable to the studio until after this is over."

"But what should we do now?" Mary Bubnik asked.

Suddenly Miss Myna flapped her wings and shrieked, "Reeeelaaax!"

"That's right, Myna," Annie said with a chuckle. "Let's all calm down and not jump to any conclusions." She squeezed Miss Delacorte's arm and whispered, "Now, come along with me, and I'll make you a nice hot cup of tea." She led a worried-looking Miss Delacorte through the curtain and out of the room.

"Thieves. Even Miss Springer believes it," McGee whispered as the girls quickly changed into their street clothes. "Who do you think could have done it?"

"Courtney probably did it to herself, just to stir up trouble," Rocky declared. She turned to Zan who was standing quietly beside the dressing table. "What do you think, Zan? You're the detective."

Zan wasn't listening. She was staring intently at the yellow piece of paper lying on the table. Miss Delacorte had forgotten to take it with her when she left. Zan picked it up and caught her breath.

"What is it?" McGee asked. "What'd you find?"

"I'm not sure," Zan replied, examining the paper in her hand carefully. "But this note may be the key to solving the mystery of who stole Courtney's necklace . . . ."

"And," McGee added, "why they're trying to frame Mary Bubnik."

"Let me see that note." Gwen held out her hand.

Zan tucked it in her pocket and lowered her voice. "We can't talk here. We need to go to someplace safe."

The five girls looked at each other and nodded. "Let's go to Hi Lo's."

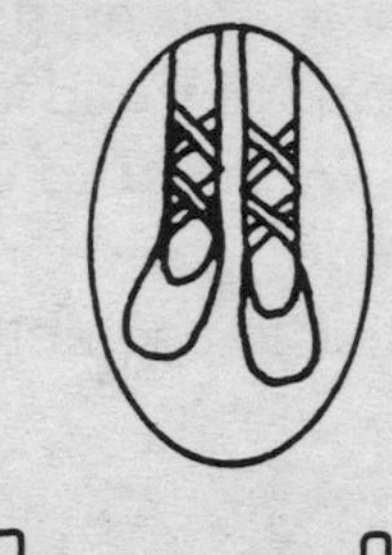

Chapter Five

"Greetings and salutations!" the smiling owner of Hi Lo's Pizza and Chinese Food To Go sang out as the gang stepped into the cozy interior of his little diner. He was busily wiping off a table in the corner of the tiny restaurant. As the girls hopped up onto the red leather stools at the counter, Hi set glasses of water in front of them. "What can I get for you ladies today?"

He was met by a line of solemn faces. McGee broke the silence first. "Nothing for me, Hi."

Rocky shook her head in agreement. "I couldn't eat a thing."

"Me, neither," Mary Bubnik agreed.

Hi arched an eyebrow at Gwen, who hesitated for

a moment, then mumbled, "I'm not hungry, thanks."

"Not hungry?" Hi's sunny face grew concerned.

"We came in to have an emergency meeting," Zan explained.

"Ah."

"I hope that's all right," Mary Bubnik said.

"Of course," Hi assured her. "Is something wrong?"

"This is the worst Saturday ever!" Mary blurted out. "My mom told me I can't take dance classes at the academy anymore." Her lip trembled as she said, "I'll probably never see you again, Hi." Mary dabbed her eyes with a paper napkin from the metal dispenser.

"But why?" Hi asked.

"Her mom can't afford it," Rocky said bluntly.

"So we have to find a way to raise the money," McGee declared. She pounded her fist adamantly on the counter top. "We just have to!"

"And so you called an emergency meeting," Hi said, nodding wisely. "A very good plan."

"But that's not the worst thing," Gwen said. "Today Courtney Clay accused—*yeow!*" Gwen rubbed her side where Rocky had jabbed her with an elbow. "Why'd you do that?"

Rocky and the others glared at her silently.

Hi looked at their somber faces for a moment, then rubbed his hands on his white apron. "My friends, you must excuse me, I have to catch up with my chores." He shook his head and hustled into the kitchen, muttering, "So many things to do, and only me to do them."

As soon as Hi was gone, Rocky turned on Gwen with eyes ablaze. "What are you trying to do, blab everything?"

"What's wrong with telling Hi that the Bunheads are up to their usual dirty tricks?" Gwen retorted.

"Please, guys, don't fight!" Mary Bubnik pleaded. "We may not be together many more times."

"Mary's right," McGee declared. "If we're going to help her, we've got to stick to business."

"We have to clear Mary's name." Zan pulled out her lavender notepad and set it on the counter. "And we're going to have to solve a *real* mystery to do it."

The girls nodded and moved in closer together.

"Here's what we know," Zan began. "The person who stole Courtney's necklace — "

"And her two Snickers bars," Gwen reminded her.

Zan nodded. "Whoever did it had to commit the crime *during* our dance class. That eliminates everyone in the classroom as a suspect — including Mary Bubnik — because we have witnesses to prove we were all together."

"So Mary's off the hook," McGee said with a sigh of relief.

Zan smiled and nodded happily. "That's right. She's got an alibi."

"Hold it, Sherlock," Gwen interrupted. "I hate to rain on your parade but we're forgetting something. Mary wasn't in the studio the whole time, remember? She came in late."

"But that's only because she went to the bathroom first," McGee objected.

"Yeah, who's side are you on, anyway?" Rocky demanded.

"Mary's, of course," Gwen shot back. "But don't you see? We can't *prove* that Mary didn't go into the dressing room and take Courtney's necklace when we all thought she was in the bathroom."

"I would never, ever do a thing like that," Mary Bubnik protested, a hurt look in her eyes.

"It doesn't matter," Gwen went on logically. "If we can't prove it, nobody will believe us. So we've got to get hard proof."

"I think we have it." Zan took out Miss Delacorte's note and unfolded it on the counter. The letters seemed to leap off the page in big, bold print:

MONDAY — 3:30. PAY BILL, OR ELSE.

"The key to the mystery is right here." She tapped the note with her fingernail. "I think that Miss Delacorte is being blackmailed by some underworld gangster named Bill. And now she's being forced to steal to pay him off. Remember, while all of us were in class, Miss Delacorte was out in the lobby all by herself. She had plenty of time to go through Courtney's bag."

"That sweet old lady?" Mary Bubnik questioned. "I don't believe it."

Rocky nodded. "She just doesn't seem the type."

"Money can make people do strange things," Zan said sadly.

"But that's not a motive," McGee objected. "Doesn't the academy pay her to be a receptionist? Why would she have to steal?"

"Wait a minute!" Gwen exclaimed. "Remember when she lost the cash box today? If we hadn't helped her find it, she would have owed all that money to the studio. What if that wasn't the first time it happened?"

"I get you," Rocky jumped in. "Miss Delacorte lost the week's receipts and had to replace the money fast, or she'd get fired. So she went to a loan shark — "

"A what?" Mary asked.

"A loan shark!" Rocky and Gwen shouted together.

"I saw it in a movie once," Rocky explained. "They're real slimy guys who lend you money and then want a lot more back than they gave you. If you don't pay up, they . . ." Rocky's voice died in her throat.

"They what?" McGee demanded.

Rocky gulped. "They kill you."

"Do you think that's what 'OR ELSE' means?" McGee asked with a shudder.

"Has to," Gwen replied. "I wonder how much she owes him?"

"We can't let this happen to Miss Delacorte." Mary's voice was tight with fear. "We've got to help her!"

"We don't have much time," Zan mused. "It says Monday."

"That's the day after tomorrow," Rocky reminded them.

"So what do we do?" McGee asked.

"I've got an idea," Zan whispered. She motioned for the others to come closer. They leaned forward with their heads together in a tight huddle. "How about — ?"

"Five specials for five special ladies!" Hi announced, bursting in from the kitchen with a platter on his arm.

The gang let out a scream of fright. Hi leaped back in alarm, almost falling into the refrigerator. "What's the matter, what's the matter?" he shouted, frantically trying to keep from dropping his dish.

"You scared us half to death!" Rocky said accusingly.

"That makes us even," Hi replied, setting the plate safely on the counter. "Because you just gave me a heart attack."

McGee looked up sheepishly and giggled. "Sorry, Hi, we didn't see you coming."

Gwen stared down at her lap in dismay. "I'm not sure, but I think I wet my pants."

"No, you didn't," Zan said with a grin. "You just knocked over your water glass." She picked up the empty glass and set it upright. McGee grabbed several napkins out of the dispenser and dabbed up the rest of the spill.

"Well, now that the excitement's over," Hi said, setting a huge bowl in front of them, "how about a world-famous Hi Lo Special Triple Scoop Bananarama Split?"

The girls gasped at the heaping mound of ice cream and fresh bananas, drenched with butterscotch syrup and hot fudge, mountains of whipped cream and sprinkles, with five cherries perched on top. Hi set five long-handled spoons down on the counter. "Dig in. It's my treat."

"Oh, Hi, you shouldn't have," Zan protested. "Besides, we're still having our meeting."

"That's why I thought of ice cream," the old man replied. "Cools the brain. Keeps it from overheating from too much thinking."

"I have to admit," Gwen mumbled, "all this mental exercise has made me kind of hungry."

"Me, too," Rocky said, staring at the sundae greedily.

"Me, three," McGee echoed. The three of them grabbed spoons and attacked the bowl with enthusiasm.

"Wow, thanks, Hi." Mary Bubnik sunk her spoon into the corner of the bowl and licked it clean. "My mom won't have to fix me dinner tonight. That'll save some money for sure."

"Any luck with your money-making plans?" Hi asked as he sat down at the corner table. He spread out a piece of poster board and began writing on it with a felt pen.

"Actually, we haven't got to that part yet," Zan admitted. "But we'll think of something."

"What's that, Hi?" McGee asked, arching her neck to see what he was writing.

"It's a sign," he explained without looking up. "I'm going to put it in the window when I'm done."

"A sign?" Rocky looked up from her ice cream curiously. "Like a menu?"

"Not quite." Hi finished his careful printing and held the poster up for them to see. It read, HELP WANTED.

"Why do you need a helper, Hi?" Gwen asked, wiping some chocolate ice cream off her upper lip with a napkin. "I mean, let's face it, this isn't the busiest diner in Deerfield."

"I'm getting too old to do it all by myself anymore," Hi explained with a heavy sigh. "I've been thinking about hiring a helper for some time." He stepped up to the window at the front of the restaurant and began taping the sign to the glass. "Of course, it's only part-time — just one day a week — and I can't pay a lot of money. So it's going to be hard to find just the right person."

"How much can you pay?" McGee asked, chasing a cherry with her spoon around the syrup at the bottom of the bowl.

"Only five dollars for about an hour's work."

"Gee," Mary Bubnik mused idly, "that's what it costs for one ballet class at the studio."

Zan and Gwen jerked their heads up at the same time. "Exactly what kind of person are you looking for?" Zan asked.

"Oh, somebody reliable," Hi replied. "But they have to be somebody I can get along with, too."

"Could they work after school?" McGee asked.

"Sure," Hi replied.

"I think I know someone who might be a good helper," Gwen suggested with a smile.

Hi turned away from the window and raised his eyebrow. "Really?"

"Someone who's easy to get along with," Gwen said.

"And who'd work real hard, if you gave her the chance," Zan added.

"Someone you know real well, too," McGee summed up.

"And, boy, does she need the money," Rocky finished.

"This sounds perfect," Mr. Lo said, leaning on the counter beside them. "Who?"

"Mary Bubnik!" they chorused.

"Me?" Mary looked up in surprise. "*Me!* Oh, gosh, Hi, I'd love to do it." She caught herself and added shyly, "That is, if you want me."

"Interesting," Hi said, rubbing his chin. "You girls may have come up with the perfect solution to my problem."

"So, I've got the job?" Mary asked hopefully.

Hi Lo went to the window and tore the sign in two. "You've got the job."

"Hurray!" the girls cheered.

"But first you have to get permission from your mother," Hi cautioned, dropping the sign into the wastebasket. "If she says OK, well, then you can start next Saturday morning before dance class, if you like."

"I'm sure she'll say yes," Mary replied happily. "And now I can keep taking lessons at the Academy!"

"Yea!" The girls all raised their spoons in a cheer.

When the gang finished their good-byes and stepped outside, Mary Bubnik was grinning from ear to ear. "Gosh, y'all, I feel so lucky. Just think, if we hadn't have come in here this afternoon, Hi might've hired someone else."

"No kidding," Rocky agreed, tying her red satin jacket around her waist by the sleeves. "What a lucky break!"

"Now if we can get Mary Bubnik off the hook for

Courtney's stolen necklace," Gwen said, "everything will be great again."

"All we have to do on Monday," Zan reminded them, "is stop this guy Bill."

"Oh, my gosh!" McGee exclaimed. "I forgot all about Miss Delacorte and the blackmailer. How're we going to stop the payoff?"

Zan smiled mysteriously. "I have an idea."

Chapter Six

"I still don't understand why we have to wear these stupid disguises," Gwen said as the gang stood huddled in the alley outside Hillberry Hall late Monday afternoon.

Zan sighed patiently. "Because Tiffany Truenote always wears a disguise when she's tailing someone. And she never gets caught."

"That's because she doesn't look like us." Rocky tugged at the loose white dress she had put on at Zan's house. The hem hung almost to her ankles. She had pulled her wild hair into a ponytail and pinned the little white cap to the top of her head.

McGee looked down at her identical white uniform and shook her head. "Yeah, I think it would have been more convincing if we'd gone with my idea."

"Now who'd believe we were five old men with beards running around on the street?" Zan asked.

"You think they're going to believe we're five nurses?" Rocky retorted.

"Correction," Gwen said sourly. "That's four nurses, and one Brownie."

"That's even worse," Rocky said.

"You're telling me," Gwen grumbled. "I still don't see why I had to be the Brownie."

"You were the only one who fit the uniform," Zan explained.

"You call this a fit?" Gwen hooted. "I'm going to have to be cut out of this thing." The buttons barely closed along the front of the high-waisted brown dress. "These sleeves are so tight that I've lost all feeling in my arms. Even the beanie is too small."

"I think the way you've got it pinned makes it look more like a nurse's cap," Rocky said.

"So why can't I be a nurse, too?"

"Gee, I'm sorry, Gwen," Mary Bubnik said, wrapping a belt around her waist. "Mom only had four of her nursing outfits in the closet. It's just lucky I found that Brownie uniform. Mom bought it at a garage sale hoping I'd grow into it."

"Grow into it?" McGee laughed. "You're already too old to be a Brownie."

"I know that," Mary Bubnik said. "But my mother

doesn't. She thinks the little beanie hats are real cute."

"I think they're embarrassing," Gwen griped. "And if anyone I know sees me in this getup, I am never forgiving any of you for as long as I live."

"Lighten up, Gwen," McGee said. "Remember, we're only doing this because we're desperate."

"That's right," Zan said. "Miss Delacorte is being blackmailed by Bill, and we've got to save her. Once we find Bill and turn him in, Courtney will know that Mary didn't steal her necklace. I'll write a story about it and win the Tiffany Truenote contest. Then I'll give the prize to Mary, and everything will be fine."

"You make it sound so simple," Rocky said.

"It is!" Zan declared. "If you take things one step at a time." She checked her watch. "Now it is exactly three o'clock. Miss Delacorte is supposed to meet Bill at three-thirty. I think we should all line up in single file against the wall."

Three nurses and a Brownie lined up behind Zan who peered around the corner of Hillberry Hall. "No sign of her," she whispered.

"I know this sounds like a silly question," Gwen called from the back of the line. "But what do we do when we see her?"

"We follow her, keeping a lookout for Bill."

"But we don't know what this guy looks like," Rocky pointed out logically.

"But we *do* know that Miss Delacorte is planning to meet him," Zan replied. "So whoever she's talking to right at three-thirty — that's Bill."

"Good thinking." McGee patted Zan on the back.

Zan smiled shyly. "Tiffany Truenote teaches you to use your powers of deduction."

"I wish I could use my powers of disappearance," Gwen grumbled. "I *hate* this costume."

"Speaking of costumes," Mary Bubnik drawled from the middle of the line, "I know I'm the one who thought of these nurse's outfits, but right now they're not much of a disguise. We just look like us."

"I worried about that, too," Zan said. "So I brought some makeup from home. This should make us look older."

She passed around a tube of lipstick and a small compact mirror. Each girl carefully applied the bright red color to her lips — including Gwen, who also drew circles on her cheeks.

"And now," Zan announced, digging in her tapestry bag, "the final touch." She held up five pairs of sunglasses in varying states of disrepair. Some of them were missing the little arm that went over the ear. One pair was held together at the nose bridge with masking tape.

"All right!" Rocky cried. "Shades." She reached for the mirrored aviator sunglasses.

"Gwen, these will go perfect with your outfit!"

McGee held up a red plastic pair that had Mickey Mouse faces on them.

The girls slipped on their glasses and turned to beam at each other.

Rocky snickered. "All we need are some white canes, and we'd look like four blind nurses — "

"Being led across the street by an aging Brownie," McGee finished for her.

That made everyone laugh, including Gwen, who was giggling so hard two of her buttons popped off her uniform. Of course, that made the gang laugh even harder.

Zan, who had been keeping watch at the corner, suddenly hissed, "It's Miss Delacorte." Everyone stopped laughing at once. Zan counted to five and then said, "All right. Follow me."

They followed Zan out of the alley and onto the sidewalk. Miss Delacorte was half a block ahead of them.

"Keep moving," Rocky ordered, running low along the ground. "You'll be harder to hit."

"What does that mean?" Mary Bubnik asked as she tiptoed in an exaggerated manner up to a parking meter.

"It means if Bill starts shooting at us, we're a moving target."

"Shooting!" Mary Bubnik gasped.

"Don't pay any attention to her," Gwen advised

from behind a parking sign. "She's been watching too many war movies."

Miss Delacorte, clutching the metal cash box, abruptly turned right and stepped inside a building with a green-and-white-striped awning over the entrance. Zan peeked over the hood of a parked car and announced, "Miss D. has entered what appears to be a newsstand and candy store."

"I'll handle this one," Gwen volunteered. She leaped onto the sidewalk, causing another button to spring off the front of her dress.

"Another quick move like that," Rocky cracked, "and you'll be arrested for indecent exposure."

"Very funny." Gwen put her hands on her hips. "I have my clothes on underneath, you know."

"That's probably why your dress is exploding," Mary Bubnik remarked.

Gwen opened her mouth to make a snappy comeback when Zan broke in, "The suspect is leaving the newsstand." She gestured for them to follow, and she hurried off in pursuit of Miss Delacorte, sticking close to the wall of the building.

"Suspect?" McGee raised an eyebrow at the others. "I think Zan's gone off the deep end with this detective stuff." Reluctantly she fell in line behind the rest of the gang. They caught up with Zan outside the entrance to an old brick building.

"She's inside," Zan whispered.

Mary Bubnik peered through the big display window. "It's a hat shop. Look, you guys, they have everything in here."

The girls lined up with their faces pressed against the glass. The tiny shop was crammed from floor to ceiling with shelves and shelves of hats. Straw hats, top hats, hats with feathers, hats with ribbons — every kind imaginable.

"Now we know where Miss Delacorte gets those weird turbans and scarves," Rocky said as they watched her try on hat after hat.

"Do you think Bill is working in here?" Mary Bubnik asked.

"It's possible." Zan was carefully writing down everything Miss Delacorte did on her lavender pad. "This could be a front for a big blackmailing gang."

At that moment a little door at the back of the shop opened, and a tiny old lady tottered up to the sales counter. She wore a pale blue smock and carried a stack of hat boxes in her arms.

"That must be the oldest lady in the world," Gwen marveled. "She's got more wrinkles than Hi Lo."

"Do you think that could be Bill?" Mary Bubnik wondered.

"If it is, that's the most incredible disguise I've ever seen," Rocky muttered.

"Look out!" McGee said. "Miss Delacorte is coming this way."

Their receptionist stepped out onto the sidewalk and adjusted the broad straw hat she had just purchased. The girls huddled in a tight clump by the window of a neighboring storefront. They stared into the vacant interior until Miss Delacorte had gone by.

Zan checked her watch. "Three twenty-five. We should meet Bill at the next stop."

"That must be Deerfield Savings and Loan," McGee called. "Because she's going inside. Come on!"

Zan tried to get them to slow down and proceed in an orderly manner but they were too excited. Rocky gathered her long nurse's dress around her waist and jogged alongside McGee. "I can't wait to see this guy."

"Me, too!" McGee huffed.

"Hey, wait for us," Gwen and Mary Bubnik shouted together.

The entrance to the bank was a revolving door and all four girls tried to crowd into one slot. The panel moved about six inches, then jammed as Gwen's shoulder became wedged against the glass.

When Zan spotted them caught in the door, she wanted to sink into the ground. "Tiffany Truenote would never allow this to happen," she murmured to herself. With a sigh, Zan braced herself against the doorjamb and shoved against the glass panel. The revolving door suddenly jerked loose and spun the gang out into the lobby in a tangled heap. The tellers and people lined up at the little windows turned to gape at them.

"Get off me, Gwen," McGee groaned, "I'm suffocating."

"I've lost my nurse's cap," Mary Bubnik cried.

"Subtle! Very subtle!" Rocky said, jerking her leg out from under McGee.

"There she is!" Mary Bubnik declared. As she smoothed out her hat, she asked, "Do you think Miss Delacorte saw us?"

"If she didn't, she'd have to be blind," Rocky replied.

Gwen grinned meekly at Zan, who stood a short distance away from them, shaking her head. "I guess we got carried away."

"I guess." Zan offered Gwen a hand up. "Come on, Miss Delacorte is in the far line."

The girls followed Zan to a tall oak table where they pretended to fill out deposit slips. McGee looked over her shoulder and whispered out of the corner of her mouth, "There are two other people in line with Miss D., but they're both women."

"Maybe the teller is Bill," Mary Bubnik whispered back.

"We'll know in a minute," Zan said. She carefully pulled her pad out of her pocket and took notes.

Suddenly Miss Delacorte, who had been standing quietly in line, patted her coat pockets nervously. She dug down in her big cloth handbag, then spun in a circle looking at the floor. Without a backward glance, she marched to the revolving door and left the building.

"That must be the signal," Zan cried. "Bill's supposed to follow her."

Miss Delacorte was moving much faster this time. She almost ran the entire way back to Hillberry Hall. The gang followed as unobtrusively as they could. They waited around the corner as Miss Delacorte scurried up the one hundred and two steps into the old stone building. By the time they got through the main door, they could hear the sound of her footsteps climbing the stairs.

"She's going into the studio!" Rocky exclaimed. "Let's go!" She started to take the stairs two at a time.

"Wait! We'd better stay here in the lobby for a second," Zan said, trying to catch her breath. "We don't want Miss Delacorte to know we're behind her."

"But won't Bill see us if we're out here in the open?" McGee asked logically. "That might scare him off."

Zan bit her lip for a moment. "You're right. Let's go up and hide. But be quiet."

Gwen, who had collapsed on the floor, gasped, "You guys go on without me. I'm near death as it is. Bill can just finish me off."

"Oh, no, you don't!" McGee cried as she and Rocky grabbed Gwen by the arms and pulled her to her feet. "This is all for one, one for all, remember?"

Gwen could only grunt in response. Rocky and McGee pulled her after the others all the way to the third floor. The hallway was pitch dark. A dim light shone through the frosted glass door of the Deerfield Academy office but that was all.

"Where is everybody?" Gwen wondered out loud. The others shushed her, and she clapped her hand over her mouth. "Sorry!"

"The only classes on Monday are for dancers in the Deerfield Ballet, but they're performing in Cincinnati today," Zan explained in a low voice. "So no one's in the studios."

"You guys?" Mary Bubnik whispered. "It's pretty scary up here with the lights off."

"Yeah, it gives me the creeps, too," McGee murmured, taking Mary's hand. "Especially if Bill's around."

Five shadows darted down the hallway and tiptoed into the darkened reception area. A light was coming from inside Studio A and the gang could hear someone walking around. Zan led them into the curtained dressing room where they waited breathlessly to see what would happen next.

The lights in the reception area flicked on and the five peeked through the crack in the curtain. Miss Delacorte was rummaging through her desk, pausing now and then to say, "Oh, no. Oh, dear. This is not good."

"This blackmailer has really got her scared," Mary Bubnik whispered.

The old woman went through her desk twice, then ransacked the file cabinets. She even walked over and peered into the ladies' room. Then she disappeared into Studio B.

"I wonder what she's looking for?" Gwen asked.

"I don't know, but she'd better find it before Bill gets here." Zan couldn't contain her excitement. On her very first case as a detective they were about to catch a criminal in the act.

Suddenly the lights on the entire floor went out. They heard a door shut from inside the studio.

"I think she just went out into the hall by the other door," Rocky hissed.

Footsteps clicked along the marble floor. The girls listened as Miss Delacorte walked up to the front door of the studio. A key rattled in the lock and there was another loud click. Then the footsteps faded away down the hall.

McGee rushed out into the lobby. The rest of the girls heard the brass doorknob rattle in the darkness. "You guys aren't going to believe this," McGee called back in an eerie voice.

"I'm sitting in the dark wearing Mickey Mouse sunglasses and a Brownie uniform with only two buttons left on it," Gwen answered. "I'll believe anything."

The doorknob rattled again and McGee announced, "This door is locked. We're trapped!"

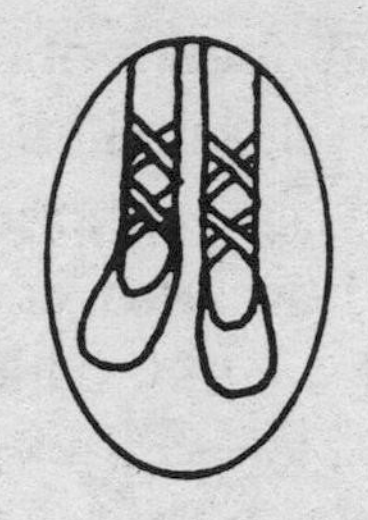

Chapter Seven

"Let us out!" Gwen shouted as she pounded on the locked door of the studio. She hoped maybe the janitor might hear them, but no one came. The building seemed completely deserted.

Mary Bubnik joined her, shouting, "It's dark in here, and we're scared!"

"Now everyone try to keep calm," Zan said, pulling a tiny pocket flashlight out of her bag. She flipped it on and a thin beam of light cut through the darkness. "There, that's a little better."

"Better!" Gwen repeated. "We're trapped in this dance studio with no food." A distant note of panic crept into her voice. "We could starve to death by tomorrow afternoon!"

"Yo, Gwen," Rocky called. "Relax. We've got a telephone right here."

Zan trained the tiny beam of light in the direction of Rocky's voice. It illuminated Rocky and McGee standing beside the black phone on the desk. Mary Bubnik and Gwen hurried over to join them. Their eyes had adjusted to the dark enough to move around without knocking into things.

"Let's call the police," McGee said, picking up the receiver, "and tell them to get us out of here."

"Hold it!" Gwen grabbed her hand before it touched the dial. "How do we explain what we're doing in the building?"

"Gwen's got a point," Rocky said. "We could be booked for breaking and entering."

"Why don't we call Hi Lo?" Mary Bubnik suggested. "He'd understand."

"Now, what good would that do?" Rocky demanded. "He doesn't have a key."

"How about Mr. Anton or Miss Jo?" McGee proposed. "They're the heads of this place — I'm sure they've got keys."

"Of course they've got keys," Gwen snapped. "But I'm not having Mr. Anton come in here and yell at me — not in this outfit. No way!"

"Besides, they're in Cincinnati with the rest of the ballet company," Rocky reminded them.

While the girls talked, Zan knelt by the front door, busily examining the keyhole.

"Get her," Gwen remarked sarcastically. "She still thinks she's Sherlock Holmes."

"Forget it, Zan," McGee called wearily. "It's locked, we're stuck — "

"And I'm starved," Gwen finished for her. "Why don't we call out for something to eat?"

"How would we get it in here?" Mary Bubnik asked.

"Easy," Gwen replied. "If we order pizza, the guy could just slide it under the door."

"Aha!" Zan cried out triumphantly.

"What is it?" McGee called, rushing over to the front door.

"We're in luck." Zan pointed at the keyhole with her penlight. "This is an old-fashioned lock that uses a skeleton-type key. Miss Delacorte left it in the keyhole."

"Figures," Rocky mumbled. "She seems to leave everything."

"But that's truly wonderful news," Zan exclaimed. "You see, we don't need to call anyone for the key. I'll get us out of here."

"How?" McGee asked. "The key's on the other side."

"Watch." Zan hurried over to the desk and grabbed a piece of white typing paper. She picked up a paper clip and straightened it out with her fingers.

"Do you really think you can do it?" Mary Bubnik whispered to Zan.

Zan nodded. "Keep your fingers crossed."

The gang followed Zan back over to the door, where she knelt down beside the lock. "Somebody hold the flashlight."

McGee grabbed it and trained the beam on the keyhole. The gang gathered round curiously. Zan slipped the sheet of paper under the door, leaving just a few inches showing on their side. Then she took one end of the straightened paper clip and carefully pushed the key out of the lock. They all heard it hit the floor on the other side with a soft ring.

"This is the tricky part," Zan muttered. "Here goes."

She gently tugged on the piece of paper, pulling it back from under the door into the office. The long brass key was resting on the paper, gleaming in the flashlight beam.

"Ta da!" Mary Bubnik snatched the key and held it up.

"We're free!" Gwen squealed with glee.

Rocky gave Zan a high five. "Way to go!"

"You're a genius," McGee gushed.

"Not me," Zan said, blushing. "Tiffany Truenote's the genius. I got the idea from one of her books."

"Then hooray for Tiffany Truenote," Mary Bubnik cried.

"I don't know about you guys," Rocky said, "but I'm not hanging around this place another second."

"Let's get out of here," Gwen urged, "before something else happens."

"Bill could be in the building," Mary Bubnik whispered.

At the mention of Bill, all five girls made a beeline for the stairs. Using the banister as a guide in the dark, they flew down the three flights of stairs and raced across the lobby out into the chilly air.

Rocky was leading the pack, and she didn't bother to stop when they were outside. She hurtled down the one hundred and two steps so quickly she didn't notice the figure huddled near the bottom step.

"Look out!" McGee cried from behind her.

"Whoa!" Without breaking stride, Rocky leaped into the air in a perfect *grand jeté* and soared right over Miss Delacorte nearly knocking her hat off. The old woman looked up in alarm. As soon as Rocky landed on the sidewalk, she ran back to the receptionist. "I'm sorry, Miss Delacorte, I didn't see you until I was right on top of you."

"Are you all right?" Mary Bubnik asked as the rest of the gang joined her.

"Lost, all is lost!" Miss Delacorte moaned, shaking her head.

The girls exchanged glances. "What's lost?" McGee asked.

"I don't know what is wrong with my mind," the old lady rambled.

"Is there anything we can do to help?" Zan sat

down on the step and patted her reassuringly on the shoulder. "If you lost something, we'd be happy to help you look for it."

Miss Delacorte placed her hand under Zan's chin and smiled sadly. "You are all so sweet. I will miss you."

"Miss us?" Gwen gasped. "Where are we going?"

"It is I who will be gone."

All five of them remembered Bill's awful threat in the blackmail note — OR ELSE. Rocky knelt down on the step below. "Please, Miss D., tell us what's going on."

Miss Delacorte forced another smile. "You are so nice to worry about my troubles. I speak to my animals about how I am getting so forgetful but, of course, they don't answer. I must be going crazy."

"I talk to my dolls all the time," Mary Bubnik said, "but that doesn't make me crazy." She looked at the rest of the gang. "Does it?"

"Not unless they talk back," Gwen said under her breath.

"Miss Delacorte, what is it?" Zan pleaded. "We can help, really."

The old woman took a deep breath. "You will not believe this — "

"Try us," Gwen said.

"I have lost the cash box again. And today I must pay bill, and I don't know what to do."

The girls looked at each other and nodded sympathetically.

"It's OK, Miss Delacorte," McGee encouraged. "We know all about your problem."

"And we think it's time to get the police," Rocky added.

Miss Delacorte's eyes widened with fear. "Police? Oh, no!"

"You can't keep paying Bill forever, you know," Gwen reasoned.

"But I must pay bill," Miss Delacorte sputtered. "The rent for the studio is due today. If I forget to pay zee bill at the bank again, Mr. Anton will kill me."

"Hold it!" Gwen commanded, thrusting her arms out. "Do you mean bill as in, 'Pay the bill, Monday?' That bill?"

"Yes."

Rocky stood up very slowly. "So you don't owe a man named Bill any money?"

"Not unless he is the man who has the mortgage on the Academy."

"And you're not being blackmailed?" McGee demanded.

"Of course not." Miss Delacorte looked confused.

They all faced Zan. "So there was *no* Bill," Gwen said loudly, "and *no* blackmail."

"I guess not." Zan remained calm. "But there is still a mystery. And if we don't solve it, it sounds like there may be a murder."

"What mystery?" Rocky folded her arms across her chest.

"What murder?" McGee demanded.

"Quit scaring me," Mary Bubnik pleaded.

"The Mystery of the Disappearing Cash Box," Zan replied. "And if we don't help Miss Delacorte find it, Mr. Anton is going to murder her."

"She's right," Miss Delacorte wailed. "Mr. Anton will never forgive me. I'll lose my job for sure."

"Think back to when you last had the cash box," Rocky suggested.

"Yeah, use Zan's memory technique," McGee urged. "It worked the last time."

"I have tried all these things," Miss Delacorte replied. "But nothing works. I do not understand. I had it clutched in both my hands when I left the studio, then — pouf! It's gone!"

Mary Bubnik raised her hand. "I think I know where the cash box is." The girls all stared at her in disbelief. "Miss Delacorte stopped at several places after she first left Hillberry Hall, right?"

Rocky nodded in agreement. "Right."

"The newsstand, the hat shop, and the bank." Mary ticked them off on her fingers as she listed them. "It's not at the bank 'cause that's where she noticed it was gone. She was only at the newsstand for a moment, and she bought a magazine, which she could have done with one hand. So it must be at the hat shop."

"How can you be sure?" McGee questioned.

Miss Delacorte's eyes lit up. "Because it takes two hands to put on a hat. I must have set it down in that store when I tried on my new straw hat." She stood up abruptly. "And now I remember exactly where it is!"

"Three cheers for Mary Bubnik!" Zan cried.

"Hip, hip, hooray!" the others shouted in unison.

"Aw, it was nothing," Mary Bubnik giggled. "I just used Trixie Truenote's powers of memory."

"That's *Tiffany* Truenote," Zan corrected.

"Oops! I forgot."

Gwen patted Mary Bubnik on the back. "I would never have believed it if I weren't here as a witness."

"But now I must go and get the cash box," Miss Delacorte announced, "so I can pay bill before the bank is closed."

Mary Bubnik scratched her head. "I thought there wasn't any Bill."

Gwen grinned broadly and teased, "Now *that's* the Mary Bubnik I know and love."

Miss Delacorte led them back down the street toward the hat shop. "It is so fortunate that you ran into me." Miss Delacorte seemed to have relaxed even though she kept up a brisk pace. "I almost didn't recognize you in your nurse's uniforms and Fudge suit."

"That's Brownie," Gwen grumbled.

"But then I thought," the old lady continued,

"there could not be four nurses that short who all know each other in the city of Deerfield."

"I told you we should have dressed like old men," McGee grumbled.

Rocky took off her white nurse's hat and jammed it in one of her pockets. "We still would have stuck out like sore thumbs."

"Are you all doing a play somewhere?" Miss Delacorte quizzed.

"Something like that," Gwen joked.

At the hat shop Miss Delacorte ducked in to retrieve the cash box while the gang waited outside.

"Well, now we're right back at the beginning," McGee said. "We're no closer to finding out who stole Courtney's necklace than before."

"I, for one, have had it with this detective stuff," Gwen declared. "This 'Pay Bill' mess is silly enough, but running around all afternoon in this dumb uniform is the absolute pits."

"Yeah, do me a favor, Zan," McGee said. "Next time you want to solve a mystery, leave me out of it."

Zan wasn't listening. She had her nose deep in her notepad. She flipped over three pages and crossed off a few lines with her pencil.

"Earth to Zan." Rocky waved her hand in front of her face. "Come in."

Zan blinked her big brown eyes at the group.

"There are still several loose ends to tie up before this case is closed."

"Well, you can count me off the case," Gwen announced firmly.

"You guys keep forgetting," Zan said, "until the mystery of the stolen necklace is solved, Mary's the number one suspect."

"Zan's right. And don't forget those Snickers bars," Rocky reminded Gwen. "You're not exactly off the hook, either."

"OK, OK," Gwen relented. "I still think Courtney snarfed those candy bars herself. I, personally, am not a Snickers girl." Her stomach growled loudly, and Gwen grinned sheepishly. "Talking about food makes me kind of hungry."

"You're always hungry," Rocky retorted as Miss Delacorte emerged from the shop. She had the cash box clutched tightly under her arm.

"Did I hear someone say they were hungry?" Miss Delacorte asked.

Gwen's eyes lit up. "Well . . ."

"Because I would like to invite you all to my apartment for tea."

Gwen couldn't mask her disappointment. "Tea?"

"And wonderful Russian cookies," Miss Delacorte added.

"All right!" Gwen cheered.

"Sounds great to me," McGee said with a grin.

"Yeah, it'll give us a chance to get out of these uniforms," Rocky agreed.

They turned back toward Hillberry Hall when Mary Bubnik cried out in alarm.

"What is it?" Zan asked.

"Aren't we forgetting something?"

"What?" Gwen demanded.

"I hate to remind you, Miss Delacorte," Mary said, "but it's way past three-thirty and you haven't paid Bill yet."

Miss Delacorte laughed. "Right, my dear Mary Bubnik. We'll stop by the bank on the way."

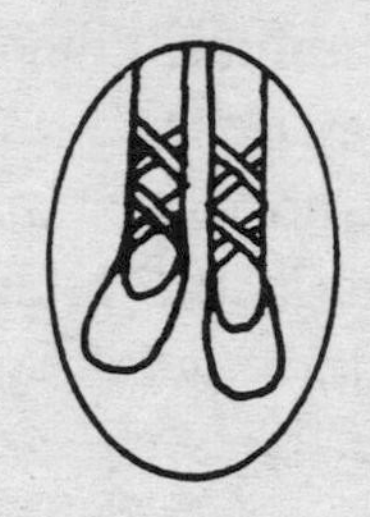

Chapter Eight

Miss Delacorte lived in an old brick building on the street directly behind Hillberry Hall. Like the ballet studio, her apartment was on the third floor.

"Doesn't anyone believe in elevators downtown?" Gwen complained as the old lady led the gang up the winding staircase. Her calves were beginning to ache from climbing so many steps in one day.

"It's good for you!" Miss Delacorte chuckled. "It keeps you young."

"If I get any younger," Gwen huffed, "I'll disappear."

"Fat chance," McGee wisecracked.

Gwen was too out of breath to respond. They reached the third floor landing and followed Miss

Delacorte down the hallway. The floor was covered with large black-and-white tiles. A brass chandelier hung down from the high ceiling to light their way. Each apartment they passed had a big curved arch over the heavy oak door. Instead of bells the doors had brass knockers in the shape of a lion's head. Miss Delacorte's door was painted a deep, dark green.

"This is truly like stepping into another time period," Zan whispered as they waited for Miss Delacorte to find her key.

"Like the Twilight Zone," Gwen replied.

"Oh, dear," Miss Delacorte murmured as she rifled through her purse and pockets. "I go through this every time I come home. I should probably just leave the door unlocked."

"My mother always keeps a spare key over the doorframe," Mary Bubnik offered.

Miss Delacorte clapped her hands together. "Thank you for reminding me. I keep mine under the doormat." She bent down and carefully removed the gold key. She unlocked the door and pushed it open. "Welcome to my home."

The first thing the girls noticed was the wonderful scent in the air. "It smells like talcum powder," Mary Bubnik cried.

Gwen sniffed the air. "And cinnamon."

"And roses," Zan added.

Miss Delacorte smiled. "It is all those things —

powder from my bedroom, cinnamon from my favorite tea, and — "

"The roses on the table." McGee pointed through the archway to a table. A fringed shawl was draped over it and a vase of roses rested on the center. To their left was the kitchen; to the right, Miss Delacorte's bedroom. Directly before them was the tiny living room.

"Pull up a chair! Relax!" a familiar voice called from the living room.

"Miss Myna!" Mary Bubnik cried.

"And friends!" Miss Delacorte hung her coat on an elaborate wooden coatrack that rested in the front alcove. "Now give me your coats and go into the living room. I will make us all some nice, hot tea."

"And cookies," Gwen reminded her.

"Oh, of course, I'm certain I have some that you will like."

Miss Delacorte's apartment was cluttered with memorabilia from her days as a dancer. A pair of faded pink satin toe shoes sat on the mantel, surrounded by old black-and-white photos in elaborate gilt frames. The girls entered the living room tentatively, in awe of the unique surroundings.

The room was dark, with heavy brocade curtains across the windows. Somehow the rich red and gold fabric made it warm and cozy. A Persian rug cushioned the floor, an antique couch leaned against the wall, and the carved oak sideboard was laden with little boxes full of letters, pictures, and trinkets. It was clear each one held a special memory for Miss Delacorte.

"This is like a museum," Rocky whispered under her breath.

"You said it, buster!" Miss Myna replied from her perch in the corner. "Awk!"

That made everyone giggle.

"Misha!" Miss Delacorte shrieked from the kitchen. "Get off the counter."

A large black-and-white cat raced out of the kitchen into the living room, followed by an orange cat with no tail. Miss Delacorte stuck her head out the kitchen door. "Meet Misha and Mr. Stubbs. Miss Myna, you already know. And there's my lovely Sasha — the oldest of them all. She was seventeen at Christmas."

An old cocker spaniel lying on a cushion beside the sofa raised her snow-white head and thumped her tail in welcome.

There was a loud clunk by the window and the curtains flew apart. A furry creature with a black mask leaped onto the big oak sideboard. He was clutching a piece of crumpled tinfoil.

"Hit the dirt!" McGee yelled, ducking her head down.

"What is it?" Mary Bubnik shrieked.

"I don't know," Gwen confessed, huddling with

Mary Bubnik in the corner. "Some sort of huge cat."

"Rudi!" Miss Delacorte cried. "You are such a bad boy! You come here, you rascal."

The creature named Rudi sprang off the table and bounded across the rug to his mistress. He raised up on his hind legs in front of her and waved his paws.

"Look, girls," Miss Delacorte said with a merry laugh, "my wicked Rudi thinks he deserves a treat for com-ink home."

"He lives here?" McGee asked.

"But of course." Miss Delacorte handed the animal a cookie, and he bounced up onto a chair to eat it, holding it in his paws and taking small bites.

"Rudi is my dearest friend," Miss Delacorte explained. "But he can be a real scoundrel. He is always running around the neighborhood."

"Doesn't he scare the other cats?"

Miss Delacorte grinned. "And dogs, too. They aren't used to seeing a raccoon in the city."

"Raccoon?" the girls shrieked.

"Is tha — that what he is?" Mary Bubnik stammered.

Miss Delacorte pointed to his face. "See that little mask that makes him look like a bandit? That is how you can tell. That, and his striped tail." She turned and went back into the kitchen.

"Does Rudi bite?" Rocky asked, inching curiously toward the raccoon.

"Only if you try to take his toys away from him," Miss Delacorte called back.

Rocky pursed her lips and made a little clucking sound. Rudi cocked his head at her, then leaped into her lap and rubbed up against her shoulder. "All right!" Rocky said softly.

As if in answer, Rudi tugged at her shiny silver necklace and licked her face.

Miss Delacorte emerged from the kitchen carrying an immense silver cannister, beautifully engraved with floral designs. A little spigot stuck out of its side near the bottom. She set it carefully on the table and moved the vase of roses to the mantel.

"Geez Louise!" McGee gasped. "What's that?"

"It is a samovar." Miss Delacorte brought in another tray laden with delicate porcelain cups and saucers. "That's a Russian teapot." Miss Delacorte turned the little nozzle and steaming, brown tea poured into the china cups. Using a pair of silver tongs, she picked up a cube of sugar and held it over a teacup. "One lump, or two?"

Everyone said one, and Miss Delacorte dropped the cubes into their cups.

Then she stirred a packet of artificial sweetener into her own cup and passed around a plate of cookies. "I hope you like marzipan."

"Mars-ie-pan?" Mary Bubnik repeated. "What's that?"

"Is almond cookie," Miss Delacorte explained.

Gwen picked up one of the small golden biscuits and popped it into her mouth. Her face broke into a wide grin. "These are great; they melt in your mouth."

Miss Delacorte looked pleased. "Have as many as you like. Rudi is the only one who eats them here." She nibbled on a saltine cracker as she talked.

"Hey, this is really weird," McGee declared from over in the corner. She was curiously examining a tall wooden box with a fluted horn on the top. McGee raised the lid and peered inside. "What is it, some kind of record player?"

"Exactly." Miss Delacorte set down her teacup and joined McGee. "This Victrola is one of my favorite possessions." There was a handcrank on the side which Miss Delacorte wound like a clock. "It was given to me by Sergei Kolnekoff. He was my first partner in the ballet." Then she carefully placed the needle on the record that was lying on the turntable.

The sound that came out of the speaker was a little scratchy at first but soon a haunting melody filled the room. Miss Delacorte nodded her head and rocked in place to the lilting music. Then she did a few steps, carefully pointing her toes, her chin held high. The music swelled, and with a graceful flick of her wrist, Miss Delacorte seemed to shed her years. For a fleeting moment, the girls could see what she must have been like as a young ballerina.

The music changed to a fast pace and Miss Delacorte clapped her hands together. "This is a traditional song from my country. Come dance with me!"

She put her hands on her hips and danced around the room. Mary Bubnik and Gwen fell in line right behind her. Zan picked up one of the long chiffon scarves draped over the couch and waved it in the air. Rocky and McGee folded their arms and, squatting on the floor, kicked their legs out in front of them like the Russian cossacks they'd seen on television.

Miss Delacorte pointed to the raccoon, who spun in a circle on the chair. "Rudi loves this music, too." After each spin the raccoon would reach across the table and pop another marzipan cookie in his mouth. But Miss Delacorte didn't seem to mind.

The music stopped and Zan and Mary Bubnik bowed gracefully to Miss Delacorte, who responded in kind. Gwen threw herself on the couch in exhaustion.

"What a blast!" McGee cried as she and Rocky sprawled backward onto the floor.

Miss Delacorte waltzed over to the table and laughed. "Look! Rudi thinks he is so clever, he has eaten all the cookies. Well, I shall just get some more." She picked up the empty plate and danced toward the kitchen. "Zan, put on another record," she called over her shoulder. "And all of you feel free to look at my treasures." She pointed to the little boxes that lined the mantel and were clustered together on the sideboard. "They just sit there gathering dust."

Zan opened a small porcelain egg. Inside the egg was a silver swan. "Look, everyone, Miss Delacorte must have danced *Swan Lake* at one time."

McGee pointed to a photo of a youthful Miss Delacorte, clad in white, with feathers on her head. "I think this is a picture of when she did it."

"She was beautiful," Mary Bubnik sighed, gazing at the faded photograph.

Gwen held up a sequined mask on a stick. "I wish we'd worn this today, instead of these silly disguises. It would have been much more dignified."

Mary Bubnik found a long pink feather boa that she wrapped around her neck. She paraded around the room with Misha the cat jumping on the trailing feathers.

Rocky noticed a simple wooden box sitting by the windowsill. She lifted the lid and peeked inside. What she found made her blood run cold.

A gold chain with a familiar trinket lay amid strips of brightly colored ribbon.

Rocky couldn't believe what she was seeing. She glanced at the others to see if anyone had noticed, but the others were engrossed with the treasures they had discovered. She turned her back to them and carefully lifted the chain out of the box. With a sinking heart she tucked it into her pocket.

"Here," Miss Delacorte sang out as she re-entered the living room, "I have found some cookies that are even more delicious than the first ones."

"Great!" Gwen made a move for the table, but Rocky was there in a flash to intercept her.

"I'm sorry but we've got to leave now," Rocky said somberly.

"What do you mean, leave?" McGee demanded. "The fun is just getting started."

Rocky shook her head. "The fun's over. I have to catch a bus, it's getting dark outside, and . . . well, we just have to go."

The rest of the girls were shocked at Rocky's brusque tone of voice.

"Gee," Mary Bubnik said finally. "If you really think we should leave. . . ."

"I do." Rocky moved to the front door.

"I don't understand." The light in Miss Delacorte's eyes faded and she shrugged. "Well, if you feel you must go, then you must." Then she smiled warmly. "But it has been a lovely afternoon. I want you all to come visit me anytime."

"We will," Zan declared. "I've truly had a wonderful time."

"Me, too!" Mary and Gwen echoed.

"Say good-bye to Rudi for us," McGee said, pointing to the raccoon, who was busy devouring the new plate of cookies.

"Oh, Rudi, you are going to get fat like a pig!"

Miss Delacorte scolded. The raccoon just clapped his paws together which made everyone laugh.

Everyone but Rocky. She stood grimly by the door. The gang put on their coats, and she pushed them out into the hallway. "Uh, thanks, Miss Delacorte," she mumbled. "We'll see you next Saturday."

Miss Delacorte waved one of her purple scarves. "I will look forward to it." She closed the door softly behind them.

Immediately Gwen turned on Rocky and hissed, "What's the idea rushing us out of there? We were having a good time."

"Yes," Zan said, putting her hands on her hips. "How could you be so rude to Miss Delacorte?"

"Not here," Rocky muttered, leading them toward the stairs. "Outside."

"What's the matter?" Mary Bubnik drawled. "Are you sick, or something? You look real funny."

"I'm sick, all right," Rocky replied as they made their way out of the old red-brick building. "But not how you think."

Once they were outside, she slumped wearily against the wall. She felt like someone had suddenly dropped a fifty-pound weight on her head. "I found out something awful."

"What?" Zan demanded.

"Miss Delacorte *is* a thief."

"No!" Mary Bubnik gasped. "We went all over that before. It was just a big confusion."

"I'm telling you, she stole Courtney Clay's necklace."

"That's ridiculous," McGee scoffed.

"I saw it with my own two eyes," Rocky shot back. "Right there in a wooden box in her living room."

There was a stunned silence. Finally Zan asked, "Are you sure?"

"Maybe it just looked like Courtney's necklace," Gwen said hopefully.

Rocky shook her head, and digging into the pocket of her jeans, pulled out a long gold chain. Dangling from the slender metal braid was a tiny dancer. It spun round and round as they watched.

"I just can't believe that sweet old lady would steal," Gwen said.

"Maybe she has an illness," Mary Bubnik said. "You know, maybe her mind goes blank, and she doesn't realize what she's doing."

"Or maybe she's a kleptomaniac," Rocky said. "Addicted to stealing."

"Oh, no!" Zan said suddenly. "I just thought of something. Now that you have the necklace, you're going to get blamed for the robbery."

"I'm not going to tell the Bunheads I have it," Rocky said. "I'm not that stupid."

"Well, then what are you going to do?" Gwen asked.

"Next Saturday, when everyone goes into class, I'm going to slip it back in Courtney's bag."

"Then you're not going to turn Miss Delacorte in?" Mary Bubnik said with relief.

Rocky shook her head. "How could I? I like her too much." Rocky stared at the little gold dancer and murmured, "Let's just hope this was a one-time thing, and she'll never do it again."

"I just can't believe she took the necklace," Zan declared adamantly. "There must be a logical explanation."

"I'll give you one," Gwen said. "She needed the money to buy pet food."

"But she has a job." Zan shook her head. "No, there must be some clue that I've overlooked."

"Clue, schmoo!" McGee said angrily. She felt betrayed by their new friend. "Miss Delacorte is a thief, and that's all there is to it!"

Her harsh words hung over the gang like a dark cloud. When they split up to go their separate ways, no one even bothered to say good-bye.

Chapter Nine

On Saturday morning, Mary Bubnik flung open the door of Hi Lo's Pizza and Chinese Food To Go. The little brass bell announced her entrance, and a moment later Hi stuck his head out from the kitchen.

"Well, if it isn't my first mate, Mary Bubnik!" Hi smiled and his face creased into a thousand wrinkles. "Welcome aboard."

Mary saluted and giggled, "Thank you, captain."

"You're just in time to help me swab the deck."

"What's that mean?" Mary Bubnik asked, taking off her winter coat and hanging it on the metal rack by the front door.

"That's navy talk for scrubbing the floor." Hi held up a mop and bucket.

Mary walked behind the circular counter. "I didn't know you were in the navy."

"I wasn't, but I've seen a lot of movies, and they always tell you to swab the deck when they want the floor cleaned."

Mary giggled again. This job's going to be fun, she thought happily. She was glad she had been able to talk her mother into letting her do it.

"Put this on and tie it tight." Hi handed her a long white apron. "It's your official uniform."

Mary looped it over her head and it stretched down over her ankles. "It seems to be a little long."

Hi folded the length in half and re-tied the apron. "There. That's much better."

Mary Bubnik ran to look at herself in the mirror that hung by the coatrack. She had to stand on a chair to get the full effect. "Gee, I look like a real chef." She ran her hands across the stiffly starched material. "Wait'll the gang sees me."

"Are they coming in today?" Hi asked, helping Mary down from the chair.

"You bet." Mary Bubnik grinned proudly. "They wouldn't miss my first day on the job! Besides, we're working on a special case."

Mary's smile faded as she thought of her friend Miss Delacorte and the stolen necklace. She shook her blonde curly head. She still believed Miss Delacorte was innocent, and so did Zan. If only they could prove it!

"Well, if we're going to have customers," Hi remarked, "we'd better finish the floor so I can show you how things work around here." He handed her the mop and held open the swinging door that led into the kitchen. "There's just one more spot that needs cleaning over by the dishwasher."

Mary dipped the mop in the soapy water and then began scrubbing the floor vigorously. "Are you going to teach me how to cook, too?" she asked, imagining herself flipping hamburgers with one hand and making milkshakes with the other.

"Maybe in the future," Hi replied. "But for today, we'll start with how to run the front counter."

Hi leaned the mop and bucket against the far wall of the kitchen and then gave Mary Bubnik a tour of the counter area. "The glasses are all stacked in the lower cupboard." He pulled out the drawer below the counter. "Here are the spoons and flatware." Then he demonstrated how to work the soda fountain. He even showed her how to dip the ice cream scoop in a glass of warm water to make it carve out the ice cream like butter.

"This reminds me of the days when I first started working for my father," Hi said, flipping the ice cream scoop in the air with a flourish.

"Was that back in China?" Mary Bubnik asked.

"No, California," Hi replied with a grin. "My dad owned a pizza parlor in L.A."

The little brass bell tinkled over the door and a man in a dark blue business suit stepped inside the diner. Hi said under his breath, "Battle stations!"

The man walked to the counter and perched on one of the worn leather stools. Mary Bubnik waited for Hi to take over, but he gave her a gentle nudge and whispered, "Go ahead. He's your first customer."

"Now?" Mary's heart suddenly beat fast. "But I'm not ready."

"Give it a try."

Mary moved to the edge of the tall counter and murmured, "May I help you?"

The man looked around to see where the tiny voice was coming from. Mary Bubnik's head barely reached the top of the counter. She raised her hand and waved. "I'm right here."

Hi came in from the back room with a milk crate and set it behind the counter. "Stand on this."

That brought Mary Bubnik face-to-face with her customer. "May I help you?" she repeated.

The man gave her a startled look. "Um, I'd like a Coke with lots of ice."

Mary carefully wrote down the order on the green pad by the cash register, then stepped off the crate. She clutched a clean glass and held it under the ice machine. Then she pressed the glass against the soft drink dispenser, taking care to not let it foam over the top. Mary grabbed a napkin and straw and stepped back on the crate. "There you go, sir. That'll be fifty cents."

The man reached into his pants pocket and placed three quarters on the counter. "Keep the change, kid."

"Gee, thanks!" Mary scooped up the money. "Be sure and let me know if there's anything else you'd like. My name is Mary Bubnik."

The man smiled. He drank his Coke quickly and promptly left the diner. "Look, Hi," Mary squealed, "I got a twenty-five-cent tip."

"Congratulations." Hi patted her on the shoulder. "You did everything perfectly. I'm proud of you."

The bell tinkled again and another man wearing dark sunglasses and carrying a briefcase came in. Following close behind was Zan. She was wearing a trench coat and carrying her trusty notepad. Zan loitered by the door watching the man intensely. He walked past the counter straight to the back booth of the tiny restaurant. As soon as he was seated, Zan tapped on the front window. The door swung open and Gwen, McGee, and Rocky came in.

"Hi, Hi!" Gwen called, clambering onto a stool. The others followed suit. Hi waved hello, then went into the kitchen. As he passed Mary, he whispered, "You're on your own."

Mary Bubnik smiled at her friends. "Good to see y'all. I just have to help this other customer, and I'll be right with you."

Zan grabbed Mary by the arm and hissed, "Be careful of that man! He's acting very suspicious."

Mary shot Zan a confused look. She picked up her little green order pad and hurried over to her customer. "Welcome to Hi Lo's. Can I help you?"

The man didn't even look at her. He just grunted and shook his head.

"Well, if you change your mind," Mary said as she backed away from him, "just holler. I'll be at the counter."

She hurried back to her friends and Zan said, "What'd I tell you? That man is truly weird."

"Don't listen to her," Gwen warned Mary. "Ever since she read about the Tiffany Truenote contest, Zan's gone mystery crazy."

"That's not true," Zan protested.

"Oh, no? Then why did you make us hide behind that parked car for five minutes so you could check him out?"

"I was just being cautious," Zan replied. "He was acting strange. And look, he hasn't even taken his sunglasses off — and we're inside."

"Maybe he has an eye problem," Gwen suggested. The gang turned to stare at the man again. As they did he placed his briefcase on top of the table, unlocked it with a key he kept on a special ring, opened it and removed two thick envelopes. Then he re-locked the briefcase and put it on the seat beside him.

Zan turned back to Gwen triumphantly. "Now you have to admit that that's strange."

"So he's going to mail some letters," Rocky spoke up. "Big deal."

Zan shook her head. "Those envelopes don't have stamps on them."

"Well, since we're here," Gwen interrupted, "I think we should all have a cherry Coke."

"Four cherry Cokes," Mary Bubnik called cheerily. "Coming right up." She was anxious to show her friends her new skills. She expertly poured their drinks and placed them in front of the gang.

Gwen took a sip of hers and pursed her lips. "Mine's missing something. Could you put a scoop of ice cream in it?"

"No problem." Mary Bubnik threw back the freezer cover and dipped the scoop into the vanilla ice cream, remembering to rinse it first in the glass of warm water. "There you go!"

McGee gave Mary the thumbs-up. "Not bad."

"You look like a real pro," Rocky added approvingly.

Suddenly Hi came racing out of the kitchen, pulling a gray sport coat over his apron.

"What's the matter, Hi?" Mary Bubnik asked.

"The Mr. Potato company was supposed to make a delivery here this afternoon," Hi muttered. "But I just saw the truck drive right past in the alley."

"Mr. Potato Head must be driving," Gwen quipped.

Hi opened the front door and peered down the street. "Typical. They're stopping in front of Peter Wong's *Golden Dragon* two blocks away." He shook his head nervously. "I've got to run and catch them. Otherwise, we'll be out of french fries by the dinner hour." Hi gave Mary Bubnik a questioning look. "Do you think you can watch the place until I get back?"

Mary hesitated. She didn't know if she could handle the place alone. Gwen spoke up for her. "Don't worry about Mary — she'll be just fine."

Hi put a plaid cap on his head. "Any customer that comes in, tell them the cook will be back in a few minutes."

"Will do," Rocky shouted.

Hi disappeared down the street in the direction of the delivery truck. Almost immediately the bell over the door jangled and this time a woman in a cashmere sweater appeared. She paused at the door and then headed straight for the man in the back booth. She, too, was wearing dark glasses.

"Oh, no, a customer!" Mary Bubnik cried in a panic-stricken voice. "I've forgotten what I'm supposed to do."

“We’ll handle this!” Gwen hopped off her stool and grabbed two red menus.

“Roger!” Rocky was right behind her with two placemats.

McGee scooped up a handful of napkins. “Don’t worry, Mary. We’ve got everything under control!”

Chapter Ten

"May I help you?"

Three girls stood facing the couple in the back booth. Each held a green pad and pencil. Each was grinning from ear to ear.

The man and woman just stared at them.

Gwen stepped forward. "Her name is Mary Bubnik, this is Rocky, I'm Gwen, and the manager's name is Hi Lo."

"As in Hi Lo's Pizza and Chinese Food To Go," Rocky explained.

"I know I asked the gentleman if he wanted anything," Mary said, "but I didn't want you to think I was ignoring you."

"I couldn't eat a thing." The woman ran her hand

wearily through her faded blonde hair. "I haven't been able to eat for months."

"Gawd," Gwen gasped, "you must be starved!"

Rocky rammed Gwen with her elbow. "How about something to drink, then?"

The woman sighed. "Yes, that would be fine."

Mary Bubnik leaned in. "What would you like?"

"I don't care, anything."

"I know the perfect thing," Gwen cried with glee. "I'll fix you a Hi Lo Special."

The woman looked at the tabletop. "That would be fine."

Gwen scribbled a few words on her pad and raced back to the counter, with Rocky and Mary Bubnik right behind her. Once they were behind it Rocky yanked Gwen by the arm. "Get down!"

Gwen ducked her head down. "What's the idea of hitting me all the time?"

"What's the idea of saying you can make a Hi Lo Special?"

"I can." Gwen stood up. "I've seen Hi do it dozens of times."

"Seeing and doing are two different things."

"Trust me." Gwen reached for two paper cups, grabbed the ice cream scoop, and went to work.

Meanwhile, Zan had not taken her eyes off the couple in the corner. She filled three pages of her lavender pad with notes.

"What're you up to?" McGee asked, giving her a nudge.

"Something's not right about those two."

"Oh, come on, Zan, I think you've got mystery mania. Everyone looks strange to you." McGee pointed casually at Gwen. "Why, look at Gwen. She's putting scoops of vanilla, chocolate, strawberry, and mocha ice cream into one tiny cup and you probably think that's strange."

Zan turned her attention to Gwen, who was smearing ice cream all over herself. "That *is* strange."

McGee sat up with a start. "You're right. It is." She leaned forward and hissed, "Gwen, what do you think you're doing?"

Gwen waved the scoop in their direction and little bits of chocolate splattered the counter. "Reeelaaxx," she said, imitating Miss Myna. "I'm making a Hi Lo Special."

"Look, she's opened her envelope!" Zan pointed to the back booth. "I'd give anything to see what's in it."

"Piece of cake." McGee held up a couple of empty glasses. "Let's take them some water."

"Good thinking," Zan said. McGee picked up a tray and Zan placed two small glasses of water on it.

"Do you think I should carry it above my head, like they do in the movies?" McGee tried to balance the brown platter but the glasses clinked together dangerously.

"I think you'd better stick to the conventional method." Zan took the tray from McGee. "Two hands. I'll carry this. You pretend to be cleaning up."

"Or how about this?" McGee picked up a bottle of ketchup and another of soy sauce. "I can pretend I'm setting up for the dinner shift. I've seen waitresses do that a lot."

"That's even better," Zan whispered. "Now follow me."

Zan moved cautiously over to the couple's table. As she set the glasses down, the man said, "Sign this and it's over." He tapped the piece of paper the woman had removed from the envelope. She didn't move but stared at it blankly.

Zan turned away and joined McGee at the next booth, her eyes two big circles. She grabbed the rag that McGee had over her shoulder and began furiously wiping off the table.

"I don't know why you want to fight me on this," the man continued.

"Because it's my life that's at stake," the woman snapped.

McGee slammed the ketchup and soy sauce down on the table and clutched Zan's arm. "Did you hear that?" she mouthed silently.

Zan nodded. She grabbed the pencil she had

tucked behind her ear and scribbled on the tabletop, "Get ready to call the police!"

McGee picked up the ketchup and soy sauce and gestured that she was going to put it on the couple's table. Zan picked up the napkin dispenser and circled around the man.

"Look, it's my life, too!" he was saying, his voice a harsh rasp in his throat.

Zan was so excited her hands were shaking. Two people, whose lives were being threatened, were sitting right here in Hi Lo's! Zan would never have believed it could happen in sleepy old Deerfield, Ohio. And she had a chance to help them, maybe even prevent a murder from happening. This was *better* than a Tiffany Truenote mystery!

Slowly Zan leaned over the back of the couple's booth, with the napkin dispenser extended, straining to catch every word. McGee did the same thing from the other side, only she was still holding the ketchup and soy sauce.

"All right!" the woman shouted. "I don't care anymore. You can have the divorce." On the word "divorce," she stood up abruptly and her shoulder snagged McGee's arm. The soy sauce spilled all over the sweater that was wrapped around her shoulders. At the same time, Zan dropped the napkin dispenser on the man's hand.

"Look out, you clumsy oaf!" the woman shrieked.

"Ouch!" the man cried. "I think you broke my hand."

"Forget your stupid hand." The woman was near tears. "Look what they've done to my sweater!"

Rocky raced over with a handful of napkins. She dabbed at the stain but it was plain to see that nothing was happening.

"We're truly sorry," Zan cried. "I don't know what to do."

McGee grabbed the sweater out of Rocky's hands. "I'll wash that out for you, I know just the thing."

She was gone before the woman could stop her. Zan and Rocky decided to join McGee rather than hang around and be yelled at. They scurried back behind the counter.

Mary Bubnik took one look at the sweater and nearly passed out. "This is just awful," she moaned. "I am going to get in so much trouble."

Rocky patted her on the shoulder. "Don't panic. That's the worst thing you can do."

That didn't comfort Mary at all. She just spun in a circle wringing her hands and murmuring, "Oh, no. Oh, no . . ."

"Soda water," Gwen yelled as she struggled to hook the paper cup full of ice cream onto the milk shake blender.

"What?" Rocky asked.

"Soda water." Gwen jammed the cup into place,

then came over to examine the sweater. "It'll get anything out. My mother says so."

"What kind of soda?" Mary asked meekly.

"I'm not sure." Gwen carried the sweater to the Coke machine and put it under the first spigot. "Let's try this." She pushed the dispenser and instantly the soy sauce spots became big brown circles.

"Stop!" Zan yanked the sweater out of Gwen's hands. "It's getting worse."

Mary Bubnik crouched behind the counter. "Everybody get down," she pleaded. "If that woman sees that she'll kill me."

"And then you'll have the murder you were looking for," McGee whispered to Zan.

"I'm not looking for a murder," Zan protested.

"Well, if you hadn't gotten so gung-ho about this mystery stuff, I never would have spilled that soy sauce on that lady."

"I don't think it's very fair to blame me," Zan replied in a hurt voice.

"Will you guys cut it out?" Rocky hissed. "We've got a crisis here and we need to solve it."

"Before Hi gets back," Mary emphasized.

"I think the only thing we can do now is wash the sweater," McGee said.

"But we don't have a washing machine," Rocky pointed out.

"No, but Hi has a dishwasher." McGee put the

sweater in her teeth and crawled on hands and knees toward the kitchen door. She was afraid to stand up and accidentally reveal the stained sweater to the couple.

Mary Bubnik crawled behind her. "I'll help you. But what if the lady asks about it?"

"No problem," Gwen called softly. "I'll distract them with my Hi Lo 'Gwendolyn Hays' Special."

As McGee, Mary, Zan, and Rocky snuck into the kitchen, Gwen stood up and beamed at the couple in the back booth. They didn't notice her. They were still arguing.

Good, Gwen thought, that gives me time to figure out how to turn on the milk shake machine. She searched the base of the blender for a button to push.

"Psst!" Mary stuck her head through the kitchen window. "We've got the, um . . . *thing* in the, uh . . . *thing.* But we need some soap. Is it out here?"

Gwen glanced around and saw a large bottle of dish detergent by the metal sink. "I've got it." She flipped on the button for the shake machine and stepped into the back kitchen. "Here's the soap!"

"Great." McGee grabbed the bottle and aimed it at the sweater. "First we put some directly on the stains." She squirted a large blue gooey amount on each of the spots.

"Just like in the commercials," Mary Bubnik giggled.

"Then we fill up the little compartment in the door with more soap, and toss the sweater in," McGee declared confidently.

Zan placed the sweater in the center of the top rack between several water glasses, then closed the door and locked the knob. "We'll set it on heavy dirt, just to be sure."

McGee hit the button and they listened to the machine roar to life. At the same moment the grinding of another machine caught their attention.

"What's that noise?" Rocky asked, moving to the window.

Gwen hit her head with her hand. "The milk shaker! It must be done." She pushed open the door and a large glop of sticky wet stuff hit her in the face. "Arrgh! It got me!"

"What's that?" Rocky gasped, backing away from the door.

"Ice cream." Gwen stumbled over the sink, pawing at her face with her hands. "It's in my eyes."

Zan stuck her head through the tiny window and narrowly missed being hit by a clot of ice cream herself. "And it's getting all over the walls!"

"What happened?" Mary Bubnik moaned.

Rocky shoved open the door and crawled behind the counter. "The shake machine shredded the paper cup," she reported over her shoulder. "It's whipped the ice cream all over the place." She reached up and turned off the blender.

"This is worse than ever," Mary said as she leaned against the counter in a daze. "Hi is really going to kill me."

McGee and Zan stood in the doorway, dumbfounded. Gwen wiped her face with a towel and said, "Who would have thought that one little milk shake could do so much damage?"

Suddenly, McGee hissed, "Geez Louise! You put a paper cup on that blender?"

"What was I supposed to use?" Gwen shot back.

"A metal cannister!"

"Well, don't just stand there!" Rocky barked. "Grab a mop or something."

Mary Bubnik raced to the utility closet and grabbed every broom and mop she could find. As she charged back out, the long mop handle inadvertently knocked the ketchup dispenser off the wall. Long streams of tomato sauce sprayed on top of her curly blonde head.

"Help!" Mary cried as she staggered back into the kitchen.

Gwen took one look at Mary's face streaked in red and screamed, "Mary's been stabbed! Call 911! Call 911!"

McGee tried to hop over the mop handle to get to the phone but tripped and fell flat on her face.

"I'm OK," Mary managed to choke out. "It's just ketchup."

"Ketchup!" Gwen dipped her finger in a glob that

had settled on Mary's shoulder and tasted it. "You're right. What's the idea of scaring us like that?"

"I didn't do it on purpose."

"Do what?" Hi called from the front door.

The whole gang turned to look at him. Mary was covered in ketchup. Gwen and Rocky had clumps of melting vanilla and chocolate ice cream dripping off them. Zan and McGee clutched mop handles and buckets.

"Excuse me!" the woman from the booth called. "Are you in charge?"

Hi could only cough.

"I'd like my sweater back. Now." The woman had her purse over her arm and the envelope in her hand. She was obviously ready to leave.

Hi looked at the gang in confusion. "Sweater?"

Rocky finally spoke up. "We're washing it. It should be done in just a minute."

Just then a gigantic puddle of soapy water crept out from under the swinging kitchen door.

"Oh, no," Gwen groaned. "Something tells me it's finished."

"Something tells me *we're* finished," McGee muttered back.

"I think we must have put a little too much soap in the dishwasher," Mary Bubnik said with a tiny chuckle. "Wouldn't you know it?"

"Dishwasher!" The woman stepped gingerly through the ice cream, ketchup and soap on the floor and demanded, "You put my sweater in a *dish*-washer?"

"Please!" Hi stepped between them. "Wait here one moment. I'm sure there has been a misunderstanding."

The woman tiptoed backwards out of the muck and drummed her fingers on the counter.

Hi was only gone for a minute but it seemed like hours. "This is awful," Mary Bubnik mumbled. "Hi's going to hate me, Courtney thinks I'm a thief . . . I don't think things could get any worse."

"Yes, they could." Gwen pointed to the kitchen door where Hi stood holding a dripping sweater. The stains were gone, but the whole thing had shrunk down to a tiny doll-size outfit.

"My beautiful cashmere sweater," the woman wailed. "I can't believe it."

"Don't worry, ma'am," Mary said, stepping forward. "I'll pay for it."

"With what?" the other girls asked at once.

"With the money I'll earn working for Hi."

"About that job, Mary. . . ." Hi gestured for her to join him in the kitchen. "Could we talk for a moment? I think we need to re-think our business relationship."

Chapter Eleven

"It sure was nice of Hi not to make us pay for that sweater," McGee said as the girls made their way into the dressing room of the ballet studio. It was an hour before class and the room was deserted.

"It was also nice of him to *let* me quit." Mary Bubnik opened the plastic bag that held her dance clothes. "I mean, I would have felt just awful if he had been forced to fire me."

"*You'd* feel awful!" Gwen dropped her canvas bag on the bench and faced her. "What about us? We're the ones who wrecked your job for you."

"Aw, you guys were just trying to help," Mary said. "But I still feel pretty bad about the restaurant."

"Come on, look on the bright side." McGee

draped an arm over Mary's shoulder. "Hi still likes us. Once we cleaned up the mess and that awful couple left, he even laughed."

"He did?" Mary smiled.

Gwen nodded and patted her on the arm. "You see? Everything's fine."

"But everything's *not* fine!" Mary Bubnik's chin began to quiver. "Courtney still thinks I stole her necklace, I still don't have any money for ballet lessons, and next Saturday is still going to be our last time together."

"But we're going to fix all that," Zan replied. "Once we solve the mystery of who stole the necklace, we'll find a way for you to stay in class."

"Mystery?" Gwen stepped behind the mirror to change her clothes. "What mystery? Miss Delacorte stole Courtney's stuff and that's all there is to it."

"I don't believe that," Zan insisted. "And I think I can prove it." She tapped her head and smiled. "Through clever deduction."

"Oh, no, not again!" Rocky moaned. "Your clever deduction hasn't exactly worked lately."

"Yeah," McGee said, slipping her leotard on over her faded pink tights. "Look what happened with that couple in Hi's restaurant. You said something was wrong with them — "

"And I was right, wasn't I?" Zan retorted. "They were getting a divorce."

Rocky pulled her jacket over her leotard and faced Zan. "But no one was trying to murder them."

"Well, I'll admit I was a little off base on that one," Zan admitted.

"A little?" the gang shouted at once.

Zan picked up her hairbrush and sat down at the dressing table. "Miss Delacorte is another matter."

"Yeah," Gwen called, "she's a *real* crook who's committed a *real* crime."

Zan slammed the brush down on the table. "That's terribly unfair of you to say, Gwen!"

Gwen stepped out from behind her mirror dressed in her snug leotard and bright pink tights. "Look, Zan, Miss Delacorte was caught with the goods. The evidence speaks for itself."

"I'm sorry, but I truly can't listen to this." Zan got up and strode to the door. "I'm going to the studio to warm up." She threw back the curtain and disappeared.

Mary Bubnik slipped on her dance shoes and followed Zan. "I think I need to be alone for a little while, too. I'll see y'all in class."

Gwen turned to Rocky and McGee, who were giving her stony looks. "All I said was the truth. Everyone's acting like I'm deliberately trying to pin it on Miss Delacorte."

Rocky jammed her hands in her pockets. "Well, you're being pretty pushy. I mean, Zan likes Miss Delacorte a lot."

"So do I." Gwen dug into her dance bag and pulled out a bag of M&Ms. "I can't help it if she's a thief."

Rocky shook her head and left. McGee followed her to the door, then turned and faced Gwen. "Maybe Mary Bubnik's lucky that her classes end next week," she said flatly. "She'll get out before our whole gang falls apart."

After McGee left, Gwen slumped down on the bench and put an entire handful of M&Ms in her mouth. For the first time in her life they tasted awful. She shoved the rest of the bag into her canvas tote and left it sitting on the bench.

Dance class was grim. The gang had placed themselves in different parts of the room. None of them felt much like being near the others. Even their teacher Annie Springer seemed to have picked up on their dark mood. She gave the class a very hard workout, as if she were trying to make up for the exercises they had missed the week before.

After the class was dismissed, Courtney stopped to talk to Annie. She pulled a towel out of her bag and draped it around her neck, leaving her dance bag open on the piano bench. Rocky spotted a chance to return the necklace she had found at Miss Delacorte's.

Rocky angled by the bench on her way out of the studio and deftly slipped the necklace into the bag when no one was looking. Then she made a beeline for the dressing room.

Inside, all the girls were busy changing into their street clothes. Mary Bubnik and Zan were in one corner and McGee stood by the dressing table, wrestling with the laces of her sneakers. Gwen slumped on the bench by the open window. Suddenly a shriek filled the air.

"Somebody stole my watch!" Page Tuttle shouted at the top of her voice.

Mary Bubnik, who was in the process of putting on her parka, froze. The whole dressing room was staring at her. She opened her mouth to protest when another anguished howl erupted.

"Nobody move!" Gwen cried from her bench. "My M&Ms are missing."

"M&Ms!" Courtney rolled her eyes in disgust. "You probably ate them in one of your feeding frenzies. You'd eat anything."

Gwen's face turned a bright shade of red, and she stared hard at her dance bag, totally embarrassed.

"Speaking of food," Rocky said, stepping in front of Courtney, "how'd you like a fist sandwich? 'Cause that's what you're going to get if you don't shut up."

The more Gwen looked at her bag, the more she realized something was very wrong. "My Twinkies are missing, too," she murmured to Rocky.

After searching through her pockets and bag again, Page walked over and confronted Mary Bubnik. "Look, that watch was given to me for my birthday," she said with clenched teeth. "I've only had it a week. Give it back!"

Mary fought hard to keep the tears from her eyes. "Page, I didn't take your watch, I swear it. If you don't believe me, you can search my stuff."

"Good idea." Courtney made a move toward Mary Bubnik, but McGee stepped in her way.

"I think we should search all our bags," Gwen declared, "because someone has definitely been in mine." She dumped out the contents of hers in the middle of the room. "When I catch who's been in my stuff, I'll . . ."

Gwen's voice trailed off as a shiny gold object tumbled to the floor. There, lying amid old gum wrappers, several empty Coke cans, comic books, and pennies, was the missing watch.

"Thief!" Page shrieked. "I'm turning you in."

"Not before I get my necklace back!" Courtney jerked the canvas bag roughly out of Gwen's hands. "Where is it?"

Gwen was in shock. She just kept staring at the shiny gold watch. "I — I have no idea how that got there," she finally choked out.

"Sure!" Page sneered, grabbing the pretty new watch and clutching it to her chest. "Tell that to the police."

"Nobody's calling the police," Rocky said quickly. "You can't prove a thing."

"The watch was in her bag," Alice Wescott said in her whining voice. "She's guilty. So there!"

"What if somebody put that there to frame Gwen?" Rocky demanded.

"Oh, really?" Page put one hand on her hip. "Who?"

"Courtney."

Courtney laughed out loud. "Now why would I do a stupid thing like that?"

"To get rid of us," Rocky shouted. "Admit it, you'd do anything to get us out of the Academy."

"What about my necklace?"

"Maybe it wasn't stolen," Rocky said. "Maybe you just pretended like it was."

Courtney crossed her arms and smiled a sickeningly sweet smile. "Then where is it, Miss Know-it-all?"

"In your own bag."

Courtney rolled her eyes at the ceiling. "I'm sure I'd steal my own necklace."

Rocky shrugged and flopped down on the bench. "If you don't check in your bag, you'll sure look guilty."

Courtney sighed and flounced over to her bag. She unsnapped it and without even looking inside, held it out in front of her. "It's not there. See?"

Page and Alice stared wide-eyed at the bag.

"What's the matter?" Courtney asked, looking at their stunned expressions.

Page didn't answer. She reached inside and pulled out the missing necklace.

"How'd that get there?" Courtney gasped.

"That's what we'd like to know," Rocky said.

"What's going on, Courtney?" Page demanded. "You didn't fake this whole thing, did you?"

"How could you do that to us?" Alice asked in a tiny voice.

Courtney's mouth opened and shut several times before any words came out. Finally she found her voice. "That necklace was not there before class. I *know* it."

"Better forget about calling the police, Page," McGee said. "Because they're going to want to know why Courtney's trying to frame innocent people like Mary Bubnik and Gwen."

"Wait a minute!" Courtney shrieked. "How did Rocky know it was in my bag? She must have put it there."

"Yeah, right," Rocky said. "I stole your necklace, just so I could put it back."

"This is all so strange." Page put her hand to her head. "I don't know what to think."

Courtney tossed her necklace in her bag and pulled the strap over her shoulder. "If you were *really* my friends you would believe me — not them."

Alice squinted at her. "It's awfully hard when you got caught red-handed."

Courtney looked at everyone in the room and realized that no one was on her side. "I hate you all," she said tearfully. "And I hope I never see you again." She stomped out of the door with a flourish.

Page and Alice looked at each other for a moment and then quietly left the room.

The gang stood staring at each other while the rest of the girls in the class filed out. After they were alone, Gwen said, "Thanks Rocky, for putting the suspicion on Courtney. They were really starting to make me nervous."

"Me, too. Thanks." Mary Bubnik smiled gratefully at Rocky.

"Aw, it was nothing," Rocky said with a wave of her hand. "Courtney deserved it."

McGee nodded. "It gave her a taste of her own medicine."

Zan took a deep breath and said, "I know you're all tired of my talking about mysteries, but I think we've most definitely got one now."

Gwen and Mary looked at each other and nodded.

"None of this is making sense," Rocky said. "If Miss Delacorte took Courtney's necklace, why didn't she take Page's watch home? Why did she put it in Gwen's bag?"

"And why would she take my Twinkies and M&M's?" Gwen asked.

"And Courtney's Snickers bars," McGee added.

Zan suddenly snapped her fingers. "That's it! It couldn't have been Miss Delacorte."

The others looked at her in confusion. "How do you know that?" Mary Bubnik asked.

Zan was too excited to explain. "Come on. I'll show you." She took two steps to the door and stopped. "But first I'll need something from you, Gwen."

"Me?" Gwen leaped back in alarm. She'd just been called a thief, and she still felt a little shaky. "What?"

"Do you have any more candy on you?"

Gwen shifted her weight uneasily. "Why? Are you hungry?"

"No, it's not for me," Zan said with a laugh. "It's for our experiment."

Gwen hesitated. "Well, I do have my last-resort extra-emergency Reese's Peanut Butter Cup in here." She held up a little zipper case that said PENCILS on it. "But I'm saving it for a desperate moment."

"I don't think things could get any more desperate than they are right now," Mary Bubnik murmured.

"I just want to borrow it," Zan said. "I promise to give it back."

McGee pried the zipper bag out of Gwen's hands. "Come on, hand it over."

"Now, follow me," Zan said, holding open the curtain. "And pay close attention."

The girls formed a line behind Zan as she led them into the reception area and up to Miss Delacorte's desk.

"Hi, Miss Delacorte," Zan called. "We wanted to thank you for the delightful time we had the other afternoon."

"Why, thank you, girls," Miss Delacorte said, smiling warmly. "The pleasure was all mine."

Zan set the peanut butter cup on her desk. "We thought you might enjoy a little candy while you're working."

Gwen panicked at seeing the last of her candy about to disappear and nearly shouted, "But eat it only if you're really hungry, OK?"

"That is so very sweet of you to offer," Miss Delacorte said. "But I'm afraid that I can't eat candy or anything with sugar in it."

"Too bad." Gwen snatched the candy off the desk before the old lady had a chance to change her mind, and stuck it in her pocket.

"You see," Miss Delacorte continued, "I am diabetic. I haven't eaten sugar since I was a lee-tle girl."

Gwen squinted her eyes suspiciously. "But what about those marzipan cookies at your house?"

"Ah, yes! They are for Rudi and Miss Myna." She smiled and said, "They love sweets."

"Just as I thought," Zan declared. She took the pencil from behind her ear, and with a great sweeping motion, crossed Miss Delacorte's name off the list of suspects.

The group said good-bye and gathered in the hall outside the studio.

"How did you know Miss Delacorte was diabetic?" Gwen asked.

"I remembered she only used artificial sweetener and never ate a cookie when we were at her house," Zan explained.

McGee leaned against the wall. "Well, it's a relief to know Miss Delacorte didn't do it."

"So she can't eat candy. That doesn't exactly make her innocent," Rocky said. "Besides, if she didn't do it, then all signs point to either Gwen or Mary Bubnik."

Gwen and Mary looked at each other and swallowed hard.

"I'm aware of that," Zan said, tucking her notepad into her bag. "And I am formulating a plan to catch the real thief." She gestured for them to come closer. "But I am going to need all of your help to do it."

Chapter Twelve

The streets of downtown Deerfield were quiet on the following Saturday morning. Even Hi Lo's wasn't open yet. McGee and Gwen were the last to arrive at the appointed meeting place outside Hillberry Hall.

"Do you think anybody will be in the studios?" McGee rubbed her hands together to keep them warm. The gang had spent the week on the phone discussing their plan, and she was eager to get started.

"I doubt it," Rocky said. "I think our class is the first one on Saturdays."

"Rocky's right about that." Zan pulled her olive-green sweater around her long, slender frame. "I was able to check the schedule, and the dance company isn't rehearsing today."

"What about Miss Delacorte?" Mary Bubnik asked. "Will she be in early to do any work?"

"We won't know about her until we get there, but my guess is that she doesn't show up this early." Rocky checked her watch. "It's oh-eight-hundred hours. Nobody should be in the studio for a while." She picked up the two extra bags she was carrying. "Besides, if she is there, she'll be at her desk while we're working in the dressing room."

"Let's get going." Gwen slapped her arms and rubbed her shoulders, hoping to warm them up. "It may be spring but it still feels like winter to me."

They scooted up the steps to Hillberry Hall. The door was unlocked, and they could see a janitor mopping the floor at the far side of the lobby.

"Act like you know what you're doing." Zan raised her chin up and marched confidently across the marble floor. The others followed suit.

"Good morning!" Mary Bubnik shouted out, lifting her hand in a friendly wave.

The janitor looked up and gave a half-wave in reply.

Rocky grabbed Mary Bubnik by the arm. "You don't have to act *that* confident. Someone might question us."

Mary Bubnik stopped at the foot of the stairs. "We're not doing anything illegal, are we?"

"Not yet," Gwen answered grimly.

The girls tiptoed up the stairs. The building was completely quiet except for the distant rumble of the furnace in the basement.

"I feel like we're secret agents on a mission," Mary Bubnik giggled.

"Or spies," McGee added with a grin.

"Try snoops." Gwen shoved her glasses up on her nose. "I can't wait for this mystery to be over so we can have normal lives again."

"Just be glad we didn't come in disguise," Rocky said. "You would have had to wear that Brownie uniform again."

Zan took out her flashlight when they reached the third floor. It was dark and the girls tiptoed down the corridor following the beam of light.

"I sure hope we catch this burglar," Mary Bubnik whispered. "I'd hate for my last day to end with everyone thinking I was a thief."

The girls turned to look at their friend. They had almost forgotten that this would be Mary Bubnik's last day at the Academy.

"Geez Louise!" McGee punched Mary lightly on the shoulder. "Don't talk like that. We'll figure something out. I'm sure you'll be back next week just as always."

"Yeah," Gwen agreed. "So just don't think about it, OK?" She dug down in her pocket. "Here, have an M&M — it'll take your mind off things."

Suddenly Zan gestured for them to be quiet. She put her ear against the Academy's door and whispered, "I hear footsteps."

Everyone cocked their head, straining to hear.

"I don't know if those are footsteps," Rocky whispered, "but someone or something is definitely in there."

Gwen shuddered in the darkness. "Maybe we should go over to Hi Lo's and wait for him to open. Then we could think this over again."

She turned to leave but McGee grabbed her arm. "Don't be such a chicken! For all we know, it could be a mouse."

"Or a rat," Rocky added.

"Then I am definitely out of here!" Gwen yanked her arm out of McGee's grip.

Suddenly the sound changed and they heard somebody whistling.

"That's some talented rat," Rocky chuckled. "Come on, let's find out who it is."

The group slowly opened the door and poked their heads into the reception area. A heavyset man wearing a dark green shirt and pants was bending over the trash can by the desk with his back to them.

"Do you know who that is?" Zan whispered.

McGee shook her head. "I've never seen him before."

Mary Bubnik stuck her head between theirs. "Maybe it's Bill."

Rocky and Gwen groaned, "There *is* no Bill!"

The man suddenly stood up and spun to face the gang. "Who are you?" he demanded. "And what in blazes are you doing here?"

The girls shrank back in alarm. The man had tangled hair that shot off in all directions from his head, with a big bristling moustache. But his most scary feature was his bushy eyebrows. They met in the middle and made him look like a real ogre. "I said, what are you doing here?" he barked. "The studio isn't open for another hour."

Mary Bubnik and Gwen clung to each other and Rocky positioned herself for a karate defense.

Zan stepped to the front of the pack. "Yes, we know. You see, we take dance classes here. Who are you?"

"The name's Jerry. I'm the new assistant janitor." He picked up the broom handle and pushed some papers into a pile. "You girls will have to wait downstairs until your class."

"But we can't!" Mary Bubnik blurted out.

"Why not?" Jerry's eyebrows arched into a long diagonal line.

"Because" — McGee shrugged her shoulders — "just because."

"Because it's Mary Bubnik's last day at the Academy," Zan jumped in, "and she has to clean out her locker in the dressing room." Zan grasped Mary Bubnik by the shoulders and held her firmly in front of Jerry.

Jerry scratched his head. "Well, OK. Just don't throw any junk on the floor. I have enough trouble picking up after the staff. Take this desk, for instance. Whoever works here must be crazy. There's paper all over the place." He peeled a little note off the side of the wastebasket. "It takes me an extra hour just to pluck these sticky little notes off of things. Take a look at this one. It says, 'Take me out.' Now, if that's not crazy, I don't know what is."

Zan stepped forward and examined the piece of paper. "Miss Delacorte's handwriting." She turned to the others and showed them the evidence.

"No wonder Miss Delacorte thinks she is going crazy," Mary Bubnik murmured. "Jerry keeps taking her notes." She crossed to the pile the janitor had neatly swept up.

Gwen joined her. "There are tons of messages here."

"Here's one to remind her to turn off the lights," Zan cried.

"And to go to the dry cleaners," McGee added.

Rocky held up another. "This one says, 'Feed the animals.' "

"Poor Miss Delacorte," Mary Bubnik sighed.

"But how could they be notes?" Jerry asked.

"They're in the weirdest places — like this one was stuck to the wall a foot above the floor."

Mary Bubnik peered at the spot next to the desk. "That makes sense. When Miss Delacorte bends over to get her purse, she sees the note."

Jerry shook his head. "I still say she's crazy."

"Well, she is a little unusual," Zan said, "but I think it might be better if you left those notes where you found them. Or at least talked to her about it."

Jerry shrugged. "I'll do that."

Rocky checked her watch and gestured for the others to go to the dressing room. "Is it all right if we go clean out Mary Bubnik's locker now?"

"Sure," Jerry replied. "Just don't make a mess."

"We won't," Zan promised.

"Miss Delacorte'll sure be relieved to know that she's not losing her mind," Mary Bubnik declared once the girls were by themselves in the dressing room.

"Yeah, Jerry's just been throwing away her reminders to herself," McGee said. "No wonder she's forgotten stuff."

"Well, that's one mystery that's solved." Zan clapped her hands together. "Now let's solve the *big* one."

Rocky set to work laying out the equipment in the two canvas bags she had brought from home. She pulled out a heavy-duty dry cell battery, several coils of electrical wire, a switch, and a box with a metal speaker on it. McGee stared down at all the paraphernalia cluttering the table. "Are you sure this is going to work?"

"You think I don't know what I'm doing?" Rocky challenged as she positioned the battery behind the free-standing mirror.

"Well, yeah, but — "

"I think we should trust Rocky," Mary Bubnik said. "After all, her dad is a security policeman at the Air Force base."

McGee nodded and handed Rocky the little speaker. "I guess I'm a little nervous."

Gwen checked her watch and glanced out of the doorway. "We've only got about a half an hour before the Bunheads show up."

Rocky cleverly ran the connecting wires along the bottom of the floorboards down the middle of the room. Unless someone was looking, they would never notice they were there. "Almost ready."

Gwen picked up the end of one of the loose wires. "What does this do, anyway?"

"It's hooked up to the switch at the battery. When the wire's tripped, it completes the circuit and the speaker makes an incredibly loud noise." Rocky grinned as she connected the switch to the wires. "I tried it last night and the neighbors thought we were under attack." She tightened one wire with a wing nut to the terminal on the battery and left the other dangling beside it. Then she sat back in the big chair.

"Is there anything we can do to help?" Zan asked.

Rocky sighed and shook her head. "Nope. I can't hook up the battery until everyone has gone into dance class."

"Well, look who's here for her last dance class." Courtney Clay swept into the dressing room, followed closely by her fellow Bunheads.

The gang was so startled by the Bunheads' sudden entrance they didn't know what to do at first. Then Rocky moved to block any view of the battery behind the mirror while Zan and the others placed their dance bags on top of the wires on the floor. Each girl took her turn to change slowly out of her street clothes into her pink tights and black leotards.

Mary Bubnik was moving so cautiously that Page Tuttle's suspicions were aroused. "What's going on here?" she demanded. "Are you stealing things again?"

"I never stole anything in my life," Mary Bubnik protested.

"Then how come you're acting so strange?" Courtney Clay walked slowly around Zan. "You're *all* acting strange. Something's going on."

Zan cleared her throat carefully. "We're just quiet

because this is Mary Bubnik's last day at the Academy, and we're going to miss her."

"Yeah, so why don't you get out of here, and let us have a last minute together?" Rocky demanded.

Courtney smiled smugly. "How touching." She crossed her eyes. "How pathetic!"

"We don't have to leave until we feel like it," Alice Wescott declared, sitting at the dressing table and crossing her legs.

"That's true." Rocky narrowed her eyes at the slight little Bunhead. "But if you stay, I might have to break your leg, and then it would be your last class, too."

Alice's eyes widened with fear. "You wouldn't dare!"

"Oh, yeah?" McGee clenched her fists and edged slowly in Alice's direction. "Why don't you stick around and find out?"

"We have more of a right to be here than you do," Page sneered, coming to Alice's defense. "After all, we're *real* ballerinas."

"Walking around like a duck won't make you a ballerina," Gwen retorted, as she popped an M&M in her mouth.

"Eating like a pig won't, either," Page shot back.

Gwen choked on her candy and leaped to her feet in anger. "Why, you — "

Zan pulled at Gwen's elbow. "Please, I don't think fighting is going to help."

"I want everybody to be friends on my last day," Mary Bubnik sniffled.

"Don't count on it," Courtney snapped. "I've told my mother about you misfits and she's going to — "

"Ladies, ladies," Miss Delacorte called from the doorway. "We can hear your voices out in the hallway. Please try to remember that you are ballerinas, not boxers." Miss Delacorte clapped her hands. "Hurry, now, you must not be late for class."

Nobody budged. Rocky and Courtney glared at each other. Finally Courtney broke away, and snatching up her dance bag, swept through the curtain. One by one the rest of the girls left the dressing room, until finally Rocky was alone.

Rocky lingered for a few seconds until she was sure no one would come in. Then she set up the trip wires to go off and, turning out the light, hurried into the studio.

"Everything set?" McGee whispered as Rocky joined the gang at the *barre.*

Just as Rocky nodded her head, the blaring sound of a siren split the air. "The alarm!" Rocky yelled. "Someone's in the dressing room!"

The gang dashed for the studio door, followed by the rest of the class. Everyone tried to get through the same door at once. Finally McGee crawled out on all fours and was the first to rush into the darkened dressing room.

A shadowy figure was lurking by the free-standing mirror. McGee lowered her shoulder and dove right into the side of the thief, knocking him up against the lockers.

"Somebody turn on the lights," she yelled, wrapping her arms around the struggling figure. "I got 'em!"

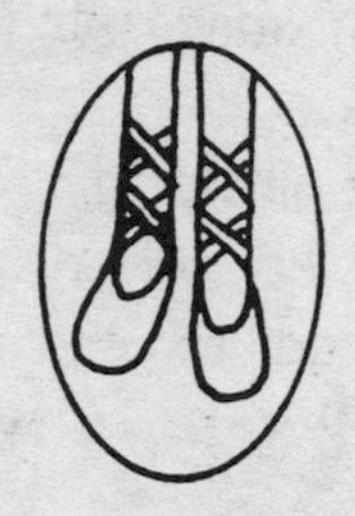

Chapter Thirteen

"Let go of me!" a female voice shrieked.

McGee struggled with the thief. "Somebody give me a hand."

"Take your grimy hands off me," the voice hollered again, twisting and turning with each yell. "You're hurting me."

"You're not getting away this time." McGee dragged the screaming person into the light of the lobby, where the rest of the dance class stood waiting.

"Oh, no!" the group cried in shock. "It's Courtney!"

Zan shook her head in disbelief. She hadn't planned on the chief Bunhead being the thief. "This isn't right," she murmured. "It wasn't supposed to happen like this."

Page Tuttle's chin quivered. "I never would have believed it in a million years."

"I knew it was her all along," Rocky barked. "This was all part of her plan to get rid of us."

Courtney struggled to stand up and McGee shouted, "Don't let her get away before we can call the police."

"You just stay away from me," Courtney ordered.

"I can't believe you'd steal my watch," Page said, her voice full of tears.

Courtney brushed off her leotard indignantly. "I never stole anything. Who'd want *your* old watch, anyway? I have a *much* better, more *expensive* one of my own."

"Then explain what you were doing in the dressing room." Gwen demanded in her best hard-boiled detective voice.

"During class." Mary Bubnik tried to imitate Gwen's tone.

"With the lights off," McGee added.

Courtney shook her head. "I don't have to tell you anything."

"That's true," Annie Springer said quietly. "But with all of the strange things going on around here, it would help if you offered an explanation."

Courtney stared at the group that encircled her. She nervously cleared her throat. "I was looking for the light switch when that horrible siren went off."

"A likely story," McGee mumbled.

"It's the truth," Courtney shot back.

"I believe her," Zan said quietly.

"Oh, no, not again!" Rocky hit the wall with her fist. "Come on, Zan, we've found the crook. I say we turn her in."

"Yeah, Zan," Gwen agreed. "How can you believe her?"

Zan shrugged her shoulders and thumped the eraser against her notepad. "Because the evidence doesn't add up, and she doesn't have a motive."

"Yes, she does," Gwen said, glaring at Courtney. "She wants us out of here and was trying to pin the robberies on me and Mary." Gwen marched over to Courtney and held out her palm. "So give me back my Twinkies."

Courtney slapped Gwen's hand. "I don't have your idiotic Twinkies."

"Thief!" McGee shouted.

"Ladies, please!" Miss Delacorte wrung her hands. "There is no reason to act like animals."

"She's right," Annie announced. "All we can do is wait and see if anything turns up missing. We can't be sure of anyone's story so there is no sense making accusations."

The room fell silent while Annie spoke but as soon as she finished, McGee mumbled, "She was caught red-handed."

"I heard that," Courtney shouted. "And it's not true! I don't have anything."

"That's because you heard us coming and put it back," Rocky answered.

In the midst of all the shouting the siren suddenly split the air again.

"Oh, no!" Mary Bubnik said, covering her ears.

Alice did the same. "It's an awful noise."

"It's the alarm!" Rocky tiptoed toward the dressing room.

Zan was right behind her. "If I'm not mistaken, we've just caught the real thief."

"I'll bet it's Bill," Mary Bubnik whispered.

"There is no Bill!" the gang hissed as one.

Rocky grabbed an edge of the curtain and yanked it back. The light from the reception area poured into the dressing room like a spotlight. There, with his hand in Gwen's bag, was a furry little creature with a black mask.

"Help!" Courtney shrieked. "It's a rat!"

Zan pointed at the raccoon and shouted with glee, "Rudi's the thief, and I've just solved the crimes."

Page and Alice clung to each other, screaming, "Get it out of here!"

Miss Delacorte pushed through the crowd. "Come here, you bad boy!"

The raccoon saw Miss Delacorte and scurried toward her, which set off another bout of screaming. This time it scared him so much that he ducked under one of the benches.

"Catch him!" Zan shouted.

Rocky lunged forward. "Quick, he's getting away!"

"Head him off at the pass!" McGee shouted as the furry raccoon raced toward the window. Rocky dove for the window but Rudi hopped onto the windowsill and was gone.

"I'm going after him." Without hesitation Rocky climbed out onto the windowsill.

McGee was quick to follow. "Me, too. We can go down the fire escape."

Annie gasped and ran for the window. "Girls! Girls! Please be careful!" She watched the two maneuver their way down the fire escape with Rudi only a few feet in front of them.

"I hope he didn't get my Reese's cup." Gwen clutched her open bag.

"My poor Rudi," Miss Delacorte cried, wringing her hands with worry, "he must be so frightened."

"Come on, Miss Delacorte." Mary Bubnik grasped the Russian woman's hand. "I'll bet Rudi's going back to your house. We can be there to meet him."

"That is such a good idea," Miss Delacorte said, hugging Mary. "Let's go."

Miss Delacorte led Mary, Zan, and Gwen out of

the studio over to her apartment, where they were joined by Rocky and McGee.

"He jumped from the fire escape over to this building," Rocky huffed.

McGee bent over with her hands on her knees and tried to catch her breath. "He's in the apartment now."

Miss Delacorte fumbled in her purse for her keys and for a moment the gang looked worried.

"Did you forget your keys again?" Gwen asked.

"They are on my desk back at the studio. We ran out so fast I forgot to grab them."

Mary Bubnik flipped up the doormat. "Then why don't you use your spare?"

Miss Delacorte opened the door and they stepped cautiously into the foyer. A patter of footsteps came running down the hallway outside.

"Any luck?" Annie Springer asked as she stepped into the apartment. "I couldn't convince the others that Rudi wasn't a rat, so they stayed at the studio. I came over to see if I could help in any way."

"Rudi? Rudi, darl-ink?" Miss Delacorte peered into the kitchen. "Are you here?"

Zan and Rocky moved toward the bedroom where they heard a crinkling sound coming from under the bed. Rocky lifted up the edge of the red-and-gold bedspread and Zan lay on her stomach to look under the bed.

"Oh, Rudi!" Zan scolded softly. "You are a little

bandit." She smiled at the four-legged thief who sat in the midst of a pile of ribbons and wrappers.

Rocky lay down beside her and gasped at the sight. "Look at all that stuff!"

"Miss Delacorte!" Zan called over her shoulder, "Rudi's in here."

Miss Delacorte hurried into the room with a cookie in her hand. She knelt beside the bed and coaxed him out into the open. "Here you go, you scoundrel, you. Come and get a treat."

Rudi scurried over to his mistress and sat up, waving his paws. Rocky took advantage of his absence to scoop up the things he had stashed under the bed.

"My barrette!" Mary Bubnik called as she came into the room. She picked up the shiny gold bar with tiny pearls around the outer edge and pinned it in her hair. "I've been looking for this for a whole month."

"And this is a brass button from Alice Wescott's coat." McGee flipped it like a coin. "It must have fallen off, and Rudi saved it."

"Here's some gold wrapping paper from the party we had for Miss Alexandra Petrovna." Zan stuck the scrap in her pocket.

"My earring!" Annie collected a cluster of ribbons wrapped around a silver loop. "I thought I lost this when the dance company was in Chicago."

Everyone rummaged through the pile that Rocky

set on the bed. They all laughed at the funny things Rudi had chosen to steal. Everyone except Miss Delacorte.

"I am so sorry, I don't know what to say. I must apologize for my naughty, naughty Rudi." She picked up the gentle pet and shook her finger at him.

"I think we should be happy our burglar is a four-legged one," Annie said, patting Miss Delacorte on the arm. "Happy, and very relieved."

"Yeah, this way nobody goes to jail," Mary Bubnik drawled.

"But I still feel so badly about all of the trouble and confusion he has caused." Miss Delacorte set the furry creature down on the floor, and he scampered off into the living room. "I will make sure that all the belongings are returned."

"I don't think everything can be returned." Gwen held up a half-dozen empty candy wrappers and two empty Twinkie bags.

"How did you figure it out, Zan?" Rocky asked.

Zan sat up on the bed. "Every time there was a robbery three things happened. The window in the dressing room was always open, candy was taken, and the jewelry was generally shiny."

"But what made you think it was Rudi?"

Zan shrugged. "The encyclopedia says raccoons like shiny things and Courtney's necklace is gold. We all know how much Rudi likes sweets. And an open window was the perfect way for him to get in and out without being seen."

"Well, why didn't you tell us this before?" Mary Bubnik asked.

"Who would have believed me?" Zan smiled. "I needed to prove it."

Miss Delacorte clapped her hands together. "This calls for a celebration. I have some cookies I can offer you." She hurried into the kitchen, and the girls heard the cupboard doors open.

"Cookies?" Gwen's eyes lit up.

"Yes," Miss Delacorte said, returning with a plate piled high with chocolate chip cookies. "I keep them for Rudi because, as you know, he has such a sweet tooth."

"Tell me about it." Gwen scooped up her wad of empty candy wrappers and dropped them in the wastebasket.

Miss Delacorte handed Gwen the plate of cookies and then turned to Annie. "Why don't you call the girls at the studio, and invite them over here for a party?"

Annie smiled. "I think that's a splendid idea. We certainly wouldn't be able to finish class." She raised an eyebrow at the gang. "And this might be the right time to make peace between you girls."

"I think that would be really nice," Mary Bubnik declared. "I'd like to be friends with everyone before I leave."

"Leave?" Annie cocked her head. "Are you moving?"

"No." Mary Bubnik shook her head sadly. "My mom made a new budget. She says we can't afford my ballet lessons anymore." Then she forced herself to smile. "So I guess this could be kind of a going away party."

Zan's and Gwen's eyes suddenly filled with tears. Even Rocky and McGee felt a little tight in the throat.

"Mary," Zan murmured, "I'm so sorry I didn't figure out a way to help you stay. I feel like I failed you."

"Now don't say that," Mary Bubnik replied, giving her a big hug. "You did your best. And I'm certain once you write the story of how you solved the mystery of the missing necklace, you'll win the Tiffany Truenote contest for sure."

"But it will be too late," Zan whispered.

McGee slumped in a chair. "I wish there was something we could do."

"I wish you could be my assistant," Miss Delacorte said wistfully. "At least some of the time. You know, when I have so much bill pay-ink and remember-ink to do." She put her arm around Mary Bubnik's shoulder. "You and I seem to think alike."

Annie, who had been listening to them, said suddenly, "I think I may have an answer!"

Mary Bubnik's blue eyes opened wide with new hope. "You do?"

"I'd have to double check it with Mr. Anton." Annie

jumped up and paced in a circle. "But I see no reason why he wouldn't go along with it."

"What?" the girls shouted at once.

"Having Mary help Miss Delacorte in exchange for free lessons."

"I would *love* that!" Miss Delacorte cried.

"Do you think he'd go for it?" Rocky asked.

"If it would help the office run smoother," Annie replied with a chuckle, "I think Mr. Anton would hire Rudi."

At the mention of his name, Rudi appeared in the door and sat up on his hind legs, clapping his paws together.

"Rudi thinks it's a good idea, too!" McGee laughed.

Annie took Mary Bubnik's hands in hers. "When I was about your age, I did the same thing. I worked one day a week to pay for my classes. I'll talk to Mr. Anton this afternoon and call you with the details."

"Oh, y'all, I'm just so happy!" Mary Bubnik smiled at her friends. "I don't know what to say."

"How about trying, 'Let's eat!' " Gwen suggested, gesturing toward the table with the plate of cookies. " 'Cause I'm starved."

"Gwen!" McGee cried. "How can you possibly be hungry when you've just eaten an entire plate of cookies?" McGee held up the empty platter for everyone to see.

"An entire plate of cookies! Tha-that's not true!"

Gwen protested. "I only had two, I swear! Just as a taste test."

Suddenly they heard a loud crunching sound and Zan whispered, "I think we can solve this crime pretty quickly."

Rocky nodded and tiptoed over to the edge of the bed. "Through careful deduction — "

"And by following all of the clues — " Mary Bubnik pointed to crumbs on the floor and giggled.

McGee slowly raised the bedspread. "I think our jury would have to say the culprit is — "

"Rudi!" Gwen dropped to her knees and peered at the furry little bandit huddled in the corner under the bed. "You give those back!"

As if in answer, the raccoon shook his head and promptly devoured the rest of the cookies.

"Hmmm!" Zan said. "We seem to have another problem. A party with no treats."

"I've got a solution," Mary Bubnik said, raising her hand. "Why don't we all go to Hi Lo's?"

"And celebrate my getting a helper," Miss Delacorte said.

"And Mary getting a job," Gwen added.

"And Zan being the best detective in all of Deerfield," McGee finished.

"Deerfield?" Rocky put her hands on her hips and declared, "The whole world!"